BRANDON: THE WILDE BROTHERS

THE BILLIONAIRE'S DESIRE

ROSE FRANCIS

Copyright © 2014 by Rose Francis

All rights reserved.

No part of this book may be reproduced in any form or by any electronic or mechanical means, including information storage and retrieval systems, without written permission from the author, except for the use of brief quotations in a book review.

This is a work of fiction. Names, characters, places, and incidents either are the product of the author's imagination or are used fictitiously, and any resemblance to actual persons, living or dead, events or locales is entirely coincidental.

ISBN: 1720989133

ISBN-13: 978-1720989134

Cover design by PAPDesign.

Poison Arrow Publishing

https://poisonarrowpublishing.com

First Electronic Edition: July 2014

First Paperback Printing: July 2014

Second Paperback Edition: June 2018

ALSO BY ROSE FRANCIS

Connor: The Wilde Brothers

The Billionaire's Assistant

Serving the Billionaire

The Tycoon's Reluctant Bride

Unexpected

The Billionaire Scoop

The Billionaire Deal

Surprise Billionaire Boss

Playing with Fire

In Hot Water

A Christmas Miracle

A Valentine's Day Surprise

A Thanksgiving Dilemma

A Tangled Web

Chrysalis

Trapped

Leap of Faith

The Lifeguard

PREFACE

Brandon: The Wilde Brothers is the second book in *The Billionaire's Desire* series—contemporary interracial romance tales starring three billionaire brothers: Alec, Brandon, and Connor.

The stories are written as standalone books, but it is recommended to read them in order to experience the full story.

PART I

RECONNECTION

CHAPTER 1

LULL

Brandon awoke to the sound of his buzzing cell phone.

He glanced over at the brunette next to him—out cold and partially covered by the bed sheet—and then checked his caller ID.

He almost shot right up when he saw the name, but controlled the urge, slowly slipping from the bed to make sure he didn't disturb his sleeping companion.

"Give me a sec," he whispered into the phone as he made his way out of the bedroom and into the kitchen, joy swelling in him.

As soon as he figured he was in the clear, he said, "Erica! What a crazy surprise! Long time, no talk."

"That's on you," Erica said. "I'm shocked you still have my name and number in your phone, and I'm not sure if I should be more offended you didn't actually lose it like I figured. Anyway, this was my last attempt to reach you and let you know I'll be coming to your neck of the woods soon—if you're still in SoCal, that is. I'm moving to L.A., so if you have the time and it's okay with your current squeeze, I figured maybe we could do lunch."

"Hell yeah. I haven't seen you in...what is it...?"

"Three years," she answered. "But who's counting? Anyway, maybe we could do a double date."

"What makes you so sure I'm seeing someone?"

"Come on, Brandon; after high school it's been like clockwork—you ignore me whenever you're in a relationship. I figure you've been in a hell of a long one, or you've been hopping around with no breaks in between since I haven't heard from you in so long; in fact, how come you're answering my call now? Did the latest one just end?"

Brandon wasn't sure what to make of Erica's tone or her words. She had said everything somewhat lightly, but he had the distinct impression he was being seriously berated.

He didn't really blame her, but she had to understand, right? Girls were so untrustworthy of each other—surely she, too, didn't like when the guy she was dating had a close female friend?

"How about you and I meet first, catch up a bit, and then do the double date thing?" Brandon said.

"Aha! I knew it. You're with someone. Anyway, let's nail down the details tomorrow. I look forward to it."

"Same here," he said, hanging up just as his bed companion made her way down the stairs to join him, wearing nothing but one of his shirts.

"Who was that, babe?" she asked, looking at him with dopey brown eyes, still foggy with sleep. Her brown hair cascaded in a beautifully messy way, making her look more attractive than she was.

"An old friend of mine. Man, it was good to hear from her—I've known her since we were kids and she'll be in town soon. Wants to do lunch."

Brandon watched Jennifer's face and thought he saw it tighten at the news, but she cheerfully said, "Oh, how cool! You guys get to catch up. When last have you seen her?"

Brandon wondered if she would think it was so cool if she actually knew what Erica looked like. Already, women had issues with just the idea of female friends. They nearly lost their minds if it was a pretty one.

"It's been a few years," he said. "We grew up together, but she went off to college in New York. We still stayed in touch though—we were pretty close back in the day, so we caught up on her school breaks. Last time I saw her was at her graduation. Three years ago."

"Aw. It's always a shame when friendships like that get taken away by adulthood, huh?"

Brandon felt defensive all of a sudden. Who said anything about his friendship with Erica being taken away?

"I mean, it's been a while, but we're still good friends," he said. "Not like we used to be, but I think she'll always be a part of my life."

Brandon again thought he caught a flash of hardness on Jennifer's face, but her words belied his eyes once more.

"Oh, good. You know I've pretty much stayed in this area since birth, so I have most of the same people around. Good for you guys being able to hold on like that, especially after...you know, everything. Anyway, I'm gonna take a shower. Love you."

She kissed him on the cheek and then took off.

Brandon felt terrible as the weight of the terms of the latest challenge with his brothers descended upon him.

Here's the twist, his older brother, Alec, had said after laying out the terms. *You have to wait two weeks before sleeping with her. And whoever gets her to say, 'I love you' first and still stays with her at least three months after, wins the title to this beach house.*

Boy, did he want that beach house.

The two-week wait seemed to torture Jennifer more than him, but once they fell into bed together, everything else was a breeze. Less than a month later, she was already telling him that she loved him.

The wait made her want him more, she later told him, and she loved how respectful he was of her, and how he didn't take intimacy casually like practically everyone else she had ever met. It made her respect him more, and probably helped her fall for him faster; he was just so different, she'd said.

Brandon struggled to keep a straight face and look sincere as she spoke to him.

If only she knew what he was up to!

He eventually came to realize that Jennifer was too nice a girl to be used like this. He had been unable to repeat her amorous words to her since she said them some weeks ago, although she let him off the hook pretty easily.

I know you probably don't feel the same way just yet, but I have to tell you how I feel—I've been bursting with it. I love you, Brandon. These six weeks with you have been magical.

Brandon let out a breath. Then again, all he had to do was be nice to her for the next two months, and then let her down gently at the end. Then Alec's Hawaiian beach house would be his.

He just hoped Jennifer never found out she was only part of a dare.

* * *

"God, you look beautiful. Come here," Brandon said as he saw Erica sitting, waiting in the diner they had agreed on the following day.

She was dressed casually, but her face was so pretty and her smile so warm that she sparkled in a way that her clothes did not matter. She had the skin of a sun-kissed California girl, her hazel eyes still warm and open. And was she thinner, too?

"Always the charmer," she said, coming up to him, and he wrapped his arms around her, holding her tightly for a moment, feeling the depth of how much he had missed everything about her—from those beautiful eyes to that seemingly reluctant smile. He resisted putting his hand in her thick, curly brown hair and cupping her head, holding her to him.

It suddenly occurred to him how well she fit in his arms against him—her tall, slim frame matching his.

She pulled away and slid back into her booth seat.

"So, you're still tall," she said as he slid opposite her.

He laughed. "Thanks," he said. "You always knew how to make a guy feel special. So, what brings you to town? Have you been in New York all this time, or...?"

"Yup. Tried to work the scene there for a bit—got in a few plays. But, of course, L.A. is where the major stuff is for the most part when it comes to acting—at least for the big screen. Or the silver one."

"So you're seriously pursuing acting now, huh?"

She looked at him like his nose was falling off. "Well, I majored in Theater for a reason. What about you? Still into moviemaking yourself? Working on becoming some hotshot director?"

He grinned, feeling a bit sheepish. "I haven't quite followed that through. Ever since..." He stopped.

"Ever since you got filthy rich, you just threw all that aside, huh? Can't say I blame you. Why do anything when you don't have to? Must be nice not to have a real passion for anything."

"Ouch. Well, that almost hurt anyway. You know very well that I have a passion for at least one thing. Listen, I thought I detected a bit of hostility from you earlier and now this...what's up, Erica?"

There was no ignoring or mistaking the storm beneath her face.

"What the hell happened to us?" she demanded.

"What do you mean?" he asked, although he knew

exactly what she meant. He had known it was coming; there was no way they could dance around it for long.

"We were so close!" she said. "You even made sure to be there for me at my graduation and then poof! You're gone. How could you abandon me like that? What did I do?"

He wasn't sure if he was ready to tackle the topic just yet, but now seemed as good a time as any. Best to just get it out of the way.

"Okay, first of all, you didn't do anything. My life changed is all. Next thing you know I'm in a relationship, and the girl's all jealous of you..."

"I didn't realize you were that weak. But I guess everything adds up."

"Meaning?"

She paused. It seemed as if she had reconsidered what she was going to say. "Just that...well if I hadn't decided to try to call you one more time, you never would have checked up on me again. You're really not attached to anything but that surfboard of yours."

He gave a half-smile. "You know that's not true. And see? You do remember my one passion; in fact, I've been working on this surfing documentary, so I guess I haven't completely abandoned filmmaking. Something like *The Endless Summer*—you know that documentary I made you watch a billion years ago? Anyway, that's what life's been like for me since...you know."

"Sounds nice. And then what are you going to do?"

"What do you mean? What do you think I absolutely need to do with my life, Erica? Do you know how many people spend their entire lives wishing and hoping and working their ass off for a partial percentage of what I have, to do pretty much exactly what I'm doing? I'll ride this wave as long as I can; there's really nothing left for me to do."

She looked away briefly. "Congratulations," she said when she looked back at him. "I just thought I meant more to you, that's all. I didn't expect you to just disappear."

"You do mean a lot to me, Erica, but you understand, right? You girls are crazy. But after that girl and I broke up, I guess I had the chance to call you up and I didn't. I'm sorry. Can we please be friends again?"

"You mean, this time, you found a girl who'll allow it?"

Brandon shrugged. "This time, I won't let her stop it. I want to show you I value our friendship, despite what you think now."

She studied him for a moment. Then she said, "Well, if we're going to be friends again, Stanley will definitely want to meet you."

Brandon bristled. "Stanley? Who's Stanley, and why do we have to meet?"

Erica giggled, her whole demeanor changing and softening, reminding him much more of the girl he knew a decade ago. Her face flushed, and her smile had no sign of the tension that had tightened her face for the past few minutes.

But Brandon found himself tightening at the way just this guy's name seemed to reduce her to a schoolgirl again.

"Stanley's my boyfriend—the one I'd be joining you on a double date with. He's my significant other. My..."

"I get it. How long have you guys been going out? Where did you meet?"

"We've been together about two and a half years. I met him when I shot a small part for this indie movie. He was the cinematographer. We're moving out here together in about a month—I just came ahead to check out some of our living options and put the deposit down."

"You know if you guys don't find the right place, you can stay with me until you've sorted it out. I mean, not with me, but in this condo I don't use much. I have one in Newport Beach."

"Thanks for the offer, but we've got this. Anyway, let's plan on that double date when we're all settled in. I'm heading back to New York in two days, but he and I will be back soon."

"Can't wait to meet him," Brandon said, hoping the words didn't sound as dry to Erica as they sounded to him as they made their way through his teeth, which suddenly seemed locked together. He cleared his throat as if it would help clear the bile building in his belly at the thought of this Stanley and what he meant to Erica. "Anyway, glad you'll be near me again. We can totally hang out; it'll be like old times. I'll catch you up on the latest surf docs, you can see mine..."

"What, are you nuts? Yeah, Stan'll love that. Let's not get confused—I'll do lunch again with you sometime but don't start thinking we'll be besties again. Friends in a very general way, yes—I didn't do all of this to never talk to you again, but we're not kids anymore. I won't cut you off completely for him like you did me, but let's be real here—there's a line."

"Is Stanley really that insecure and jealous? Come on, why would he be jealous of me? We've known each other since we were kids. We're practically brother and sister, for Christ's sake."

She gave him a look, not bothering to answer verbally. But with such a look, she didn't have to.

CHAPTER 2

STAGE FRIGHT

Had Brandon lost his mind? Why would Stanley be jealous?

Oh, let me count the ways: because you're fucking hot, for one, she answered Brandon silently, although she would never say such a thing out loud to anyone. Besides, Brandon already knew; she had no doubt about it. Forget the part about him being charismatic and all those millions he made—even before he came into cash, girls flung themselves at him pretty much since junior high when he suddenly shot up six inches in height and his shoulders broadened, and he bulged muscles and veins, oozing masculinity and testosterone.

She was powerless against his charms back then, too.

Second of all, Stanley, nearly twenty years his senior, barely maintained a lower six-figure income—a solid amount, sure, but weren't all guys a little put off by another dude with more stuff? Didn't they all feel some kind of way about some guy richer than them? Especially a non-relative in their girl's life?

Thirdly, this hunky friend of hers had known her since she still had her milk teeth, from the day she and her mom moved next door to his family. That's something Stanley could do absolutely nothing about. How can you make up for nearly twenty years of friendship? All those memories she and Brandon made in the most formative and impressionable times of their lives—from camping in the front yard to hanging out in a tree house—there was no equal in adulthood once obligations started settling in. And then there were a few other memories she dared not share with Stanley, or else he likely wouldn't ever want to meet him, and might not want her to continue their connection either. Those other memories from their adolescence would have to stay between the two of them.

She wondered if Brandon had ever shared any of those stories with his temporary bed-warmers. Did those memories come back to him every now and then like they did to her?

Erica tried to keep her composure as she hugged Brandon goodbye. She tried not to think about how good it felt to have his arms around her and have her body pressed against his hard, warm one, and how easily she melted against him. Her heart ached at having to leave him again and to go along with pretending to be blasé about finally seeing him after three long years. She had to pretend that she hadn't missed him as much as she had and that she wasn't more hurt that he had changed his number and never passed the new one on to her; she had to figure out how to find him from someone else.

Why had he bothered to keep her number when he obviously had no intention of using it?

She couldn't look at him as his arms left her body, and she realized that she was looking away when his rumbling voice said, "Hey," making her look up at him.

"I look forward to your return," he said, arresting her with his blue eyes—whirlpools she had found herself lost in more than once.

She discovered the spell he could cast with those eyes ten years ago—a hypnotic gaze leaving her feeling like she never wanted to look away.

They were sitting on the bed in her room, cards displayed between them after she taught him to play Gin Rummy. She was about to gather the cards up for another game when he suddenly said, "Your eyes are really pretty." She looked up at him. "They're sort of brown, but sort of green. I don't really see eyes like that often," he continued.

Erica felt like she would melt right into a puddle.

What was he doing talking about somebody else's eyes when his should be outlawed? His stare captivated her to the point that whatever his next move would be, she could only go with it. It wasn't fair that his eyelashes were so full; there was no resisting those gorgeous blue eyes of his.

Still staring at him, she suddenly she felt like she was on a flight—like her ears had clogged up. Her heart beat so fast and loud that she would have been embarrassed had she been able to register anything but what was happening between them.

She had dreamt of this moment countless times, and

now, here it was—Brandon Wilde's lips were coming toward hers.

When their lips finally met, she had no doubt heaven existed and that she had suddenly been transported to it. She never wanted to come back to Earth.

Erica shook off the memory and began preparing to leave the diner, her eyes staying away from Brandon.

"Let me know if you need a ride back to the airport or anything," she heard him say. "In fact, do you need a ride to your hotel now? I can take you."

You sure can, she thought and then cursed herself.

She glanced at him and shook her head, smiling wide. "Brandon, I've got it handled, don't worry."

She hoped he couldn't see that she was lying through her teeth. She just knew that she couldn't be in any small space with him, despite him having a girl, and despite the fact that he hadn't made a single move on her. But in her gut, she knew she couldn't get in his car, and that she definitely couldn't risk him walking her to her hotel room; she couldn't trust herself around him.

"Thanks, though. See you," she said, waving, departing quickly.

She made sure to stop at a clothing store to pretend she was browsing, giving Brandon time to leave the area and not see her get in a taxi later.

Once in the taxi, she sat staring out of the window, wondering if it was a good idea to meet up with him again after all since he still rattled her after all these years. They had always operated as innocent friends—despite that one experimental kiss—but the way her body responded to him even now went far beyond friendly feelings, and felt too much like what she felt for him back when she had braces and frizzy hair.

She wondered what kind of girl he was with now. Probably someone like the dancer types he hung out with in school.

Then she realized she was being silly getting so worried about the whole thing. If she stuck to double dates with him, having Stanley and Brandon's current squeeze around would probably help stunt her feelings; Brandon couldn't possibly affect her as much with two other people flanking them—too much interference. Therefore, they would easily be able to interact as innocently as they used to.

Maybe the double date experience would be like getting past opening night for a play, and every time she saw Brandon after that, she'd get less and less nervous on stage. Pretty soon, she'd be able to breeze through the performance, easing into autopilot and convincingly act like what she felt for him didn't go past friendship at all.

Maybe, like most acting parts eventually, she'd go beyond playing and temporarily become that character.

* * *

STANLEY'S FACE lit up as she entered their small New York apartment a few days later, and he turned away from his desktop computer to watch her enter.

"Sorry I couldn't grab you from the airport—just got back from that shoot."

"Oh, no problem. What's a cab ride?"

"So you found the one out there?" he said, adjusting his glasses as he stared at her with rounded eyes.

Erica was struck for a moment, and then realized Stanley was talking about their new apartment.

"Oh. Well, yeah. For now, I guess. Now I know you liked the one in Burbank, but in person, the one in Studio City is so much better—I think that's the one. A little spacier, too—or at least it feels that way; they're both just around eight hundred square feet."

"It will feel like a mansion after this," he said, indicating their tiny apartment.

"And we're paying much less," she added. "The main thing we'll have to get used to..."

"Besides all that sun and open sky?" he said, grinning. "And, oh boy—those palm trees."

She thought he was so adorable sometimes—especially when he grinned like that, like a big kid. And with those glasses and his straight brown hair with the one stubborn cowlick—just looking at him sometimes made her smile.

Erica grinned back at him. "The traffic," she continued. "That's the main problem, in general. And the public transportation system isn't that great. And I know we said we'd share a car for a bit, but with me auditioning, and you with the various gigs you pick up..."

"We'll figure it out, love."

She smiled again. "I'm sure we will. Oh, my friend, Brandon, offered us a place to stay if we needed it."

Stanley's face transformed almost comically, his already large eyes behind his glasses widening. "At what cost?"

"Free, I guess. He doesn't use the place, apparently. Some condo in Orange County. Not sure where he's staying right now."

"How rich is this guy if he has empty condos around and won't charge us?"

Erica shrugged. "He and his brother won the Ultra or Mega Lotto or something. One of the highest pots ever—six hundred million or so."

Stanley's eyes bugged out again, and Erica stifled a giggle at his uninhibited shock.

"There are three of them," she continued. "Brothers, I mean. Maybe they split it three ways, maybe just Brandon and his twin, Connor—I don't know; either way, he's obviously got millions to spare."

"Wait, what do you mean you don't know? I thought you guys were pretty close?"

Erica shrugged again. "We were. But honestly, the last time I saw him was at my graduation. He showed up and everything was normal. Then later that summer, the lottery thing happened. Haven't heard from him since."

This time, Stanley's face transformed to outrage. "I didn't realize it was *that* asshole you were planning to see! Why on earth would you even want to reconnect with a guy like that? What kind of person just drops an old friend without a second thought? I mean, you didn't even ask him for money or anything, right?"

"Of course not! I didn't even know what had happened until his number changed and I started asking around about him. Never was able to reach him. You were around when I tried again some months later—you remember. Anyway, I recently added someone on my

Facebook who has Connor as a friend—although he's not under his real name—and through him, tracked Brandon's new contact info. Connor had no problem passing it on; he remembered me."

"Again, why go through all of this trouble for someone who clearly no longer wanted anything to do with you?"

Erica tried to ignore the pain in her chest at the words spoken so plainly and so full of truth.

"We had such a long history, you know?" she said, feeling injured and a bit defensive. "And now that we'll be sort of in the same geographic vicinity again, I thought I could at least find out what happened. I...I had to know."

Stanley's face relaxed in understanding. "I get it. Unfinished business."

Erica nodded. "I guess."

"So did he tell you what happened?"

"He blamed some relationship he had going at the time—a jealous girlfriend."

When Erica looked at Stanley again, she couldn't tell exactly what was going on behind his eyes, but he looked particularly intelligent and focused.

"Anyway, he mentioned interest in a double date. What do you think?" She smiled at him, hoping to diffuse the intensity of the past few moments.

Stanley's body seemed to relax as he finally turned his face back to his computer. "Sounds fine to me. We'll arrange it when we get there. I'd definitely love to meet him."

CHAPTER 3

MAKING WAVES

Stanley. What kind of name was Stanley anyway? What was this guy, eighty years old?

Brandon felt like a personal affront had been made against him. How dare Erica drop news like that on him out of the blue? Then again, what did he think, that she had joined a convent?

Brandon had never imagined what kind of guy Erica might date before. He had never seen her with one or even thought of her belonging to someone else. He had never heard of her being seriously into anyone all the while he had known her; in fact, he had the distinct impression she only pretended to get over her crush on him once he got with his first girlfriend, Tara, when they were about fifteen.

Erica talked with him about Tara like any friend would and was never mean about her or anything, but he still sensed something almost wistful about Erica after that, whether they were talking about Tara or not.

Erica was such a bad liar—her eyes gave her away every time. And the rest of her body language did too. With every too-wide smile and every excited request she made for details, Erica was lying, pretending like his new relationship didn't bother her. She always seemed a bit too happy when he came over, and her eyes a bit too open —almost drinking him in when they settled on him.

She acted like she wasn't hurt when she extended an offer of friendship to Tara and Tara barely acknowledged her.

Erica was probably still in love with him, he figured, and this guy, Stanley, was just lucky to be there for her in the meantime.

Brandon caught himself.

What the hell was he thinking? In the meantime for what? He had no intention of being with Erica himself. What was wrong with him?

Protective big brother instinct for an old friend, he decided. *I just need to feel this Stanley guy out—make sure he's good for her and being good to her. That's all there is to it.*

* * *

"So how was it? Just like old times?" Jennifer asked, smiling wide at him, her skin glowing as it usually did when she returned from a spa. At times like these, he almost thought she was beautiful.

"She was kind of mad at me actually, so we had to sort that out."

"Oh?"

"I pretty much haven't talked to her in three years; I never bothered to try to reach her."

"Oh no! Well, it's understandable she would be upset. Glad you guys figured it out." Jennifer reached up and kissed him on the cheek.

Brandon turned his head a bit to kiss her on the forehead and watched her light up.

Guilt flooded him again.

Whatever Jennifer felt for him was real—whether it was infatuation brought on by the life he led, his exterior, or whether she actually cared about him as a person, this girl felt a need to look after him.

The guilt stuck with him for the rest of the day. No matter how many times he told himself he was doing Jennifer a favor and that she would at least have this time to look back on fondly—a time when she could live like a princess if she wanted—he started to have doubts about whether or not she would actually think the tradeoff was worth it after all, considering the emotional investment.

He kept getting the feeling that even without all of his money, Jennifer would want to be with him, and that ultimately, she would ditch all material belongings in a heartbeat to own his heart.

"Hey babe, what do you think of a double date?" he asked her.

"Sounds great! Is this with your friend and her boyfriend?"

Brandon bristled at the word 'boyfriend' again. "Yeah."

"Awesome. So cool you guys are able to reconnect."

Brandon felt awful again.

Jennifer was a decent girl. She still worked hard, volunteered, and didn't even take advantage of everything available to her through him. She didn't demand trips to Paris, New Zealand, Morocco. She didn't walk him into jewelry stores and ask him for the most expensive thing there. She didn't insist he only take her to five-star restaurants.

Now he wished he had done all those things for her so she could at least comfort herself with the material things she gained after they were no longer together.

Maybe he would surprise her with a trip to Rome, a place he knew was on her bucket list. He had only flown her out of the U.S. once.

It was the least he could do.

* * *

For the rest of the day and part of the next, Brandon had trouble shaking his encounter with Erica. He fought against his desire to hear her voice again for as long as he could, but his urges overwhelmed him.

He found himself dialing Erica's number.

Relief flooded him when she answered.

"What's up?" she greeted him, and disappointment spread through him at the casual tone.

What has gotten into you? It's how you answer the phone yourself—what more do you expect from her?

"I know you're leaving soon. Wanna grab a bite to eat or something before you go? You can tell me more about the plays and stuff you did in New York, or I can show you my documentary..."

"Thanks for the offer, but how about we do that when I get back? I have a lot of stuff to finish up here. We'll have all the time in the world to catch up on the little things once I return."

"Well, if you guys need any help moving..."

"Thanks again, but we have it all sorted out."

Brandon felt another stab of disappointment.

Why did her rejection cut him so deeply? He hadn't even been the one to make this move toward reconciliation! But ever since she filled his vision the day before, he had been unable to purge her from his mind—unlike three years ago. Back then, when they made promises to see each other soon as he was about to fly back to California and she had decided to stay in New York, once his life changed, it took him a while to even think of her.

She had been one of the first people he wanted to call as soon as everything happened, but once Alec heard about him winning the jackpot with Connor, Alec got his legal team involved and they advised them not to breathe a single word to anyone. Not yet anyway—not until they had figured out what they wanted to with the money and how they wanted to do it.

Brandon was warned about various scenarios—how friends became enemies, the sudden appearance of 'long-lost' family members. He and his brother were informed of some of the many ways strangers, family, and friends alike would try to part them from their money. *Keep a low profile*, they were advised, and sitting on the news turned out to be quite easy for him, but he was never quite sure about Connor.

Then all of a sudden, his old high school girlfriend, Tara, reappeared in his life.

In high school, Tara was a dream, and all the guys wanted her. When Brandon finally got her attention in tenth grade, he couldn't believe his luck. Then again, the way that girls had started responding to him and Connor, if he'd had a bigger ego at the time, he would have known she would eventually come to him; while Tara was the girl all the guys wanted, he and Connor were the guys all the girls wanted, so naturally, they would find each other. He lost his virginity to her and all of his senses around her. She was the most beautiful creature in the entire school, and the envy of many, as a member of the cheer team.

Connor started dating her sister just because he liked the idea of two sets of twins dating each other.

"It fits!" Connor had said, grinning widely. "And look at us—the babies we would make. Hitler would love it."

Brandon needed no convincing to be with Tara—with those killer, tanned legs, the always-in-place honey-blond hair, those beautiful, large blue eyes—she was a real-life Barbie with better proportions. Everything about her fit perfectly.

Then she broke it off with him for some guy on the football team—the school's rising star.

Brandon never imagined he could hurt so much from losing someone, and he couldn't believe how easy it was for Tara to drop him like that. He thought that he would never get over how empty his life felt without her, but

Erica helped him through everything. Erica's eyes were always filled with concern, and she was always ready with a hug and got him to laugh. Eventually, he was able to feel like some semblance of himself again. In a few months, he was dating someone new—a cute brunette from the choir. Then a few weeks later, another girl—this time, a swimmer. He kept rotating every few months, and Tara soon became a faded memory. Part of him still ached for her, but it turned into a dull ache—one that continued to fade until he thought she had been banished from his heart. That is, until the summer he won the lottery and she coincidentally managed to track him down, wanting to try to be together again.

She didn't let on knowing about the money—she just said that she'd had time to reevaluate things and realized she had made a mistake letting him go.

"I'm sorry I was such a dodo head," she said when they met up for coffee. "But you know how it is. It was high school; we were teenagers. We're in our early twenties now—adults—and you know how you look back on things? I realized I made a dumb move, the move of an immature girl. Danny was the next logical choice for me and everyone was pushing for us to be together since we were so much alike—at the top of our groups and all that." She shrugged her still-lovely shoulders.

Brandon was struck by how beautiful she still looked, although it had only been about three years since he had last seen her at their high school graduation. She kept her honey-blond hair long and was still fit and toned, and everything he once felt for her came rushing back.

The next thing he knew, they were back together,

and he was doing everything he could to make her stay. Anything she asked for, he gave to her—including cutting off contact with one of his oldest friends.

Even if she truly didn't know about the lottery, he showed his hand with all the ways he tried to buy her love. But despite the expensive gifts and the trips all over the world, a year later, she left him again, once more for someone with a higher status—some billionaire broker she had gained access to as a result of being with him. Her whole social circle had changed because of him, and he was left wondering if she had planned it.

Now here he was, with a woman who operated in the opposite manner, yet he couldn't find it in him to give Jennifer the devotion he had felt for Tara.

Poor Jennifer. Maybe he'd try to stay with her beyond the terms of the challenge and see if he could develop something real for her. She deserved his best effort.

* * *

"It's Erica," Jennifer said, bringing his phone toward him.

He realized she had gotten a bit more bold about touching his stuff, and he had to stifle the desire to say something to her about checking his phone. Did all girls get so proprietary at the three-month mark?

He decided he needed to remind himself to be a bit more careful about leaving important, private stuff around. Three months was not enough time to trust this girl with access to all of his life. Although she didn't know the password to his phone, computer, safes or anything, he still needed to be smarter about keeping her locked out; he didn't really know her—she could still disappear one day with some of his belongings. Maybe she was biding her time for the best moment to rob him blind.

"Hello?" he said, picking up the call.

"So when do you guys wanna meet up? Stan and I are all moved in now and need a warm welcome."

I've got a warm welcome for you.

Brandon forced a cough to cover the beginning of what he had been about to say. He glanced guiltily at Jennifer. "Welcome to LaLa land, Erica. I'll get right on it."

Brandon tried to suppress the image his words had cooked up in his brain as he imagined himself on top of her.

Christ, what was getting into him? Why was he being attacked by all of these sexual urges and images when it came to Erica all of a sudden? Why did the very mention of her name turn his emotions on a dime?

She's a girl, you're a guy, and you're both attractive and young. Feelings of attraction are practically inevitable at some point—especially when you've known each other nearly all your lives. Just try not to think about what it was like to have her boobs squashed against you as she hugged you...

"I'll call you back when it's all arranged," he said and then ended the call. He turned to Jennifer. "Hey babe, do you have a preference? Favorite restaurant?"

Jennifer cracked a small smile. "I'm good with whatever you pick, hon."

He couldn't stand the way she said 'hon' but he

appreciated her flexibility. No doubt, if it had been Tara, she would have not only told him which restaurant they'd all be going to, but which table she wanted to sit at. On top of that, she would dictate the time, which car they'd go in—she'd have preferences for everything.

Brandon decided on a place and then made sure the time and day were okay with everyone.

Then he thought about what to wear.

He hated suits tremendously, but he would make sure he looked a lot nicer than usual—a white dress shirt maybe, with a light blue jacket, and a crisp pair of jeans with dress shoes.

Erica would probably stare at him in shock, having seen him in a T-shirt at his dressiest, and he looked forward to seeing her mouth hanging slightly open at how well he cleaned up when he walked in.

Erica had refused his offer to pick her and Stanley up in a limo; she decided to meet them at the restaurant instead, and again, Brandon had to try not to take the rejection personally.

As he entered the restaurant with Jennifer, Brandon almost missed the moment he had been unable to stop himself from picturing—Erica's pleasant surprise at his cleaned up appearance—as he spotted her in a fitted red dress, wearing red lipstick, and with her hair pinned away from her face in some old pinup style with a flower.

He realized his own mouth probably hung open and that he was probably near drooling, so he quickly closed it and moved his eyes to her companion.

"You must be Stanley," Brandon said, extending his hand and taking in the older gentleman. He tried to guess his age: forty-two? Forty-six? He had a few grays in his hair, and his eyes had long lost the luster of youth. Everything about his demeanor said old. Was Erica seriously dating a guy their parents' age?

"I've heard a bit about you," Brandon continued, still trying not to look at Erica.

"Well, I've heard a lot about you," Stanley said warmly as he shook his hand, his blue eyes huge behind thick glasses. Why would he wear those things? Didn't they get in the way of his work? Why didn't he get laser surgery or something?

"I can imagine," Brandon said. "She and I have known each other so long. Erica wasn't too hard on me, I hope."

Stanley only grinned, closed-mouthed.

"Good to see you again, Erica," Brandon said, finally turning to her and opening his arms. They hugged somewhat awkwardly—at least, it felt awkward to him since he felt so self-conscious.

He breathed her in for a moment, enjoying her various fragrances—whatever she washed her hair with, whatever she sprayed herself with, and then, just her underneath it all.

They pulled away quickly.

Then Erica turned to Jennifer and gave her a warm smile that tugged at his heart, followed by a quick hug.

"So nice to meet you, Jennifer. I've heard good things about you!" she said convincingly.

Brandon sent her another smile in gratitude. Then he looked back at Stanley.

"Everything's all set up to go on my tab, so don't try

anything," he said with a quick wink. "Just feel free to order whatever you want. Don't think twice about anything."

Erica flashed him a sweet smile and he knew that every single penny spent would be worth it.

CHAPTER 4

BLOCKING

"...So by the age of twenty-one, there we were, suddenly millionaires. Our brother, Alec, made his first million when he was in college, and when he dropped out, we figured we didn't need to go to college at all, and that we'd sort of follow in his footsteps—although personally, I'm not a techie like Alec—Connor is better at cooking stuff up so I just go along; he's a good imitator. Anyway, Alec had been fooling around with making apps since he was like twelve or so, and later, a couple of his apps went big. It just snowballed from there. He thinks he's not lucky like us, but this one gaming app started it all for him, and he did a couple of successful spin-offs. Then luck struck again when he tried something new with more practical purposes—some app for taking calls while driving or something. He also started this social network that quickly got bought out by one of the biggies—maybe to shut it down. Either way, he has a knack for making things other people want to buy off of him or invest in right away."

"So your brother works hard, but you and your twin hit the jackpot. Either way, one lucky family," Stanley said with a smile.

Erica could tell that Stanley was interested in the discussion, but she sensed that part of him was uncomfortable.

"I guess we are. Connor and me, definitely. But my brother and I had moderate success with our own app before the jackpot. Alec spent a day showing us part of his process, and once we got the gist of it, Connor and I bounced around ideas for a while, and then developed this one game. It did okay—nowhere near any of Alec's. Then yeah, bingo! Good thing Alec was successful before us, because we got some good contacts through him and got great advice. I guess we still got lucky with a few of those early investments too. We must have been tortured like hell in a previous life for the kind of ride we got in this one." Brandon smiled, pausing a moment. Then he said, "So what do you do again?"

"I'm a cinematographer."

"That's awesome, man. I had interests along those lines when I was younger—maybe not specifically a cinematographer; I mean, you just kind of point and shoot, right?"

Stanley kept a semblance of a smile while his brow crinkled. "Not exactly—definitely a bit more complicated than that. The cinematography can make or break a movie."

"Oh, I'm sure—like any other aspect, right? Cast the

wrong actor or hire the wrong director and the movie doesn't stand a chance. Hey, did Erica tell you about this movie we shot together?" Erica's eyes snapped to Brandon. "So we were like, thirteen," he continued, "and my mom knew about my moviemaking aspirations, so she bought me this camcorder for my birthday. Anyway, one day, Erica and I plotted out this whole story, and I made her act out most of it." He suddenly looked at her questioningly. "I wonder if that's when you got the acting bug? Anyway, she'd probably die of embarrassment if she saw it now," he said, looking back at Stanley.

"You don't still have it, do you?" Erica asked him. "That thing should be burned."

But despite most of her agreeing with the sentiment, part of her hoped that it still existed, that this piece of their lives—that beautiful moment in time when they were mostly together, even if not exactly in the way she wanted—had been preserved. She had a glorious time shooting that movie, and considered that summer one of the best in her entire life.

"I definitely wouldn't add it to my résumé if I were you," Brandon said to her. "And I wouldn't add it to my reel. I mean, obviously, it was fun back then, but we were kids. We can probably still laugh at it, but I wouldn't put anyone through watching that. It's probably awful."

"Well? Do you still have it or not?"

Brandon shrugged. "It might actually be in my crap somewhere, I don't know. You're right—it's probably time to go through all my stuff again for some seasonal cleaning. Speaking of cleaning, did Erica tell you about this time we spilled..."

* * *

Stanley was doing a stellar job of feigning interest, but Erica saw Jennifer's weariness with all the stories about her and Brandon in their youth quite plainly.

"Brandon, can I talk to you for a sec?" she interrupted his latest anecdote. "Can you guys excuse us?" She looked from Stanley to Jennifer as she stood and didn't wait for an answer.

Once they were outside, she said, "Brandon, what the hell are you doing in there?"

"Something wrong with talking about careers, money, and our past as kids?"

Erica gave him a look. "None of it felt as innocent as you just made it sound. Luckily, Stanley did not take you up on your invitation to butt horns."

"Look, I'm just testing the guy out. You can know a man by his actions and reactions. And the way he reacted —or didn't—was telling. You know I'm just looking out for you and making sure Stanley's the right kind of guy." He paused. "So you're into geriatric dudes, huh? Why do you like him?"

"Because he's not you."

When she saw hurt crawl onto his face, she quickly said, "I didn't mean it like that. Stan is serious, you know? Responsible, reliable—all the things I want in a guy I'd like to settle down with. So what if he's not the best-looking or the youngest, but he does what he needs to do. He works hard, he cares about his work, and he cares about me."

"Yeah, but what about when he's sixty and you're

forty, huh? What're you gonna do when he dies and leaves you alone?"

"Brandon! What a horrible thing to say! You're being a real dick right now—any of us could die at anytime from anything, you know."

"Sure, but get real—he's your dad's age! Or probably somewhere around there, I'd imagine."

"Nice, Brandon. Keep digging. I definitely want to think about the dad who left when I was three right now. Go on."

"I'm sorry. You know I didn't mean anything by that. I'm just saying that this guy's way too old for you. Aren't you a little creeped out? You're twenty-four, and he could literally have a daughter somewhere the same age as you. You want to date a guy willing to bang his daughter?"

"Brandon! You sound one hundred percent insane right now. I am not Stanley's daughter!"

"You don't know that for sure. I'm just saying—imagine this was ten years ago. You're telling me have no issue with some thirty-four-year-old guy going after a fourteen-year-old?"

"Brandon, you know that's not the same thing!"

"You may technically be an adult now, but he's still got twenty years of experience on you; he's still taking advantage of your youth." Brandon let out a sigh. "You have to dump him, Erica."

"Okay, excuse you? I don't know what you smoked or snorted before you came here, but this is ridiculous. Everything you're saying is absolutely ludicrous!"

"Not this though: listen, you'll get bored. He'll drain the life from you; I can't let that happen."

"But Brandon, it's not really your concern."

"How could it not be?"

"Look, he's a nice guy and he loves me, and that's the most important thing."

Brandon shrugged. "Sometimes that's not enough."

"So what's the alternative you're suggesting here?"

"You should be with someone who makes you feel alive, not someone who makes you die a slow death. You're young. Don't dry up early."

"Who's this guy who will make me feel alive, Brandon, and where is he? Look, until you have him standing by, ready to introduce to me, stay the fuck out of my love life. You need to mind your own goddamned business. And speaking of Jennifer, what if I had decided to go in on her in there, would you appreciate that? Answer me! You wouldn't want me to do the same to her, would you? Start nitpicking her?"

"It's not the same," he bellowed. Then he let out a short breath. "I don't really care about that girl, Erica—not like I care about you. You're actually a part of my life; she's just here for a short ride."

"Wow. Does she know that?" Erica asked, unable to process the mixture of joy and disgust going through her at his words.

"Of course she does. She's just hoping for otherwise. But this thing with her ends in less than a month."

"Wait, why so specific?"

Brandon let out another breath. "My brothers and I—we've had this dare thing going for the past few years—since we got flooded with money. We eventually got kind of bored with the girls in our new circle, so we started picking specific types to go after for a bit to shake things up. Long story short, I'm only dating Jennifer so I can win Alec's beach house in Hawaii."

Everything in Erica soured. "Are you serious? Brandon, please tell me you're pulling my leg right now."

"Dead serious, Erica," he said, but his voice had gone soft, and the look on his face seemed regretful as he watched her. "No one's gonna get hurt. I mean, she might be a little, but it's not like I'm leading her on or anything; we're just dating. Everyone does this—kicks it with someone for a while until they can't kick it with them anymore and need someone new. Rinse and repeat. I just get something solid out of the deal; we both do."

Erica held her hand up. "Just stop, Brandon. You're despicable."

He looked struck. "Don't say that, Erica."

"Let's just go back inside. God, I thought...I don't know what I thought. But you disgust me. Haven't you ever cared deeply about anything but surfing? I know this thing with me and Stanley isn't about you caring about me at all—it's about you wanting me all to yourself for selfish reasons. You just don't want anyone to play with your toys even though you never use them."

She led the way back inside, fuming, unable to get over the fact that after all this time, Brandon hadn't changed a bit.

She had ignored this side of him for the most part, but every now and then, even she couldn't look past it.

She remembered the first time she really saw the not-so-nice part of him—when she was at over at his place at a rare time he was home alone.

They were about fifteen at the time, and his mom had gone grocery shopping, Alec was out, and Connor had left to go to a neighbor's house.

It was a Saturday, and after talking about their week at school, Brandon stared at her, locking his eyes with hers and she felt the familiar hypnotism begin.

"I want you to do me a favor," he said.

Anything, she almost said, but instead she asked, "What is it?"

"I heard the average is six inches, and I want you to help me measure it."

"Excuse me?" she asked, her voice almost sounding like a screech. She knew her eyes must've bugged out, too.

"Touch it," he said. "Measure it, I mean. With your hand. That's about six inches, right?"

Her heart punched her rapidly from the inside. Still, she managed to say, "So you have a stiffy right now, and you want me to..."

"Don't get flattered or anything, it has nothing to do with you—it just does that sometimes. But since you're here..."

"Why don't you take a ruler to it sometime when I'm not here? Since it's always happening anyway."

His smile not only returned but widened.

He lowered his voice. "You know you want to. You're curious."

All she could think was, *Damn him and that stupid, new sexy voice of his with those stupid muscles coming from those stupid broad shoulders that popped up out of nowhere over the stupid summer...*

She reached her hand out and touched it, lining her hand up with his penis.

He burst into laughter and she pulled her hand back right away.

He continued laughing hysterically and shame flushed her cheeks. How could she be so stupid?

"You actually touched it!" he said, howling with laughter, seemingly unable to open his eyes from amusement at her expense as tears squeezed out.

"You better not tell anyone!" she said, just as he was saying, "I can't believe you touched it!" again.

She stormed out to go home and didn't answer his phone calls for the next two days.

Not long after the incident, she heard that he had started dating some girl named Tara, and the news made her feel even more embarrassed.

* * *

"That was awkward," Stanley said once she and Brandon sat back down at the table.

Erica watched Jennifer examine Brandon silently and then turned to Stanley.

"You know what I was telling you about before?" she said. "It was kind of boiling up in me; I couldn't get past it or ignore it. I just had to ask him about it and get more details."

Stanley nodded in understanding as she expected. He had made it clear to her that he thought her need to get the bottom of why her friendship with Brandon went sour was perfectly reasonable; he got why she didn't just accept 'jealous girlfriend' as an excuse.

"I'll tell you more about it later," she added.

Jennifer was still looking at Brandon questioningly, although Brandon hadn't yet turned to look at her. Finally, Brandon smiled at her, tapping her on the knee.

Watching Jennifer's response made Erica feel guilty —the girl was obviously smitten with Brandon and hung on to his every action, each charity smile.

Erica wondered if that's what she looked like to everyone ten years ago when she looked at Brandon.

She felt guiltier for thinking of Brandon in an improper way even once when they had lunch at the diner a month ago, the way her body responded to him, still.

"Well, I enjoyed those stories you told of my Erica when she was younger," Stanley said, his voice interrupting her thoughts. "She sounds as adorable then as she is now." He paused a moment, then said, "I have a story for you too. You know, she thinks we first met on some indie film, and technically, we did, but I actually met her months before that."

Erica turned to look at Stanley. This was news to her.

"I first met her while she sparkled on stage for a play. It was her first part out of college," he continued. "I learned that part later. Anyway, this play ran for a few months, and I happened to see it one night, and man, as soon as I saw her, I fell in love with her. She was magnificent," he said, punctuating the words. "I'm sure she has grown leaps and bounds since your kiddie videography days. She was so compelling that I came back to watch her again and again."

Erica sat, stunned. She had no idea someone had been so moved by her—her part wasn't even a leading role.

Her mom had come to see the play one night, so she knew she had an admirer then, but all the other nights, when she kept hoping and praying Brandon would show up, surprising her with a visit in response to one of her many messages—calls, emails, texts, voicemails, instant messages on social networks—she figured she had no supporters. Every single night she looked for one response, any response to: *If you're ever in town, I'm in this play I'd like you to see.*

Then Brandon's number changed altogether, and she couldn't find anyone who knew his new number. Even his social networking profiles disappeared.

She had tortured herself wondering if it was because she had kissed him on the cheek when he was leaving the day after her graduation. *It was only a friendly kiss on the cheek!* she argued with herself one of the many times she found herself lost in thought. Friends always did things like that—she didn't mean anything by it. Did he think she was going to want more from him?

"I figure this is as good a time as any," Stanley continued. "Our surroundings are stunningly beautiful—like Erica herself—and one of her oldest and most cherished friends is here, back in her life again. It just feels like the right moment."

Everything in Erica went still.

Stanley turned fully toward her. "Erica, like I said, it

was pretty much love at first sight when I saw you lighting up that stage. You're a beautiful woman, so I'm sure a lot of men probably feel that way when they first see you—you practically glow."

Suddenly, Erica couldn't take her eyes off of Stanley; in fact, she couldn't do anything. Her arm didn't even feel like hers as Stanley took it and lifted it, holding her hand.

With his other hand, he reached into his pocket and her eyes locked on the location.

"Erica, I have made no secret of my plans for you—as in, I mean to keep you. You inspire me. You make me feel vibrant. All I want to do is keep you happy and watch you blossom in the industry and find success as I know you will; no one can deny your talent. And you are a woman of many talents."

Erica found herself blushing, her cheeks warming.

Stanley pulled out a beautiful, sparkling ring, the diamond seeming to catch all lights.

She watched as Stanley held the shimmering piece at the tip of her finger.

"Erica Cain, make me the happiest man on earth—say you'll marry me. I love you, and I want to spend my life doing just that—loving you. Not just adoring you as you deserve, but doing things that show you how much you mean to me every single day. I promise to show you how much love is an action verb."

A sound coming from Brandon's side of the table finally broke the spell, and when Erica briefly looked in its direction, she thought she caught Brandon rolling his eyes.

As she turned to look at Stanley's face again, ignoring

both the ring's brilliance and the feel of Brandon's gaze on her, her heart melted at Stanley's sincerity and open-eyed devotion. She had no doubt that he meant every single word he'd said, and she knew that he was exactly what she needed—at least one form of dependability.

"Yes, Stanley," she said, bringing his hand up to kiss the top of it. When she saw his face transform into joy, she knew she had done the right thing.

He slipped the ring on, grabbed her into a hug, and then kissed her lips briefly. Then he turned to the couple opposite them, a huge smile on his face.

There was no doubt that Brandon did not share his joy. Everything about him was tight, and only when Jennifer pushed his chin up to close his mouth did his body seem to relax.

Then Jennifer said, "Oh my god, how wonderful! Can't believe we got to see that!"

Brandon turned toward Jennifer, and then looked back at them, his mouth in a semblance of a smile.

"Congratulations," he said, raising his wine glass and tipping it toward them.

Erica couldn't stop staring at how the top half of his face didn't at all match the bottom or his light tone.

His eyes were burning.

CHAPTER 5

AMPED

Brandon felt the wind get knocked out of him as Stanley proposed. When it came back, and he felt himself breathing again, the air was tainted with offense and disgust.

He watched in horror as Erica accepted the flimsy proposal and felt bile rise in him at the sight of their mutual joy.

He couldn't believe his eyes. He even blinked them a few times and wriggled his toes to make sure he hadn't drifted off into some strange daydream.

This can't be happening. Not his Erica. Not to this guy.

What kind of ring was that anyway? What a tiny little joke.

He wondered if Stanley was packing like the ring and if Erica was satisfied.

Why are you thinking that? She's like a sister to you, for Christ's sake!

But by now he knew that he was lying to himself. He wanted Erica in the biblical sense; he pulsated with a need for carnal knowledge of her. He wanted to touch all parts of her body and run his tongue down her smooth skin. He wanted to ram it down her throat. He wanted to put his mouth over her nipples, dip his fingers between her legs and tease her with all of his tips—his fingertips, the tip of his tongue, the head of his...

"Brandon?" he heard as if from far away. Then he realized that Jennifer had squeezed his thigh, breaking the bubble of the sexualized violence swelling in him.

He turned to smile at her briefly.

"So," he said, looking back at Erica. "Any idea of a date?"

Erica shook her lovely head, her eyes sparkling. He hated how happy she looked.

"No idea whatsoever. What do you think, babe?" she said, looking at Stanley.

Brandon bristled at the word and even more at the way they looked at each other.

Stanley shrugged. "All up to you."

Her smile widened.

Brandon forced himself to smile too. "Champagne is obviously in order," he said, getting a server's attention. "And how about another treat from the dessert menu? Come on, Erica, you know how much you like chocolate cake."

Erica shook her head. "Thank you, but I've grown past that."

Brandon felt personally insulted, however irrational.

Besides, who the hell grows past chocolate cake? What a silly thing to say.

He glanced at Jennifer and noticed her looking ridiculously happy for the couple. What was up with that? She didn't know any of them like that to be so delirious with joy. Was she drunk?

"You take care of her," he said to Stanley, despite feeling dried up, surprised the words even managed to make it out of his suddenly parched mouth.

Stanley locked eyes with him and said, "I will."

Brandon wondered if he was seeing things or if there was a flash of a challenge or warning in his eyes and tone. Some sort of assault anyway.

To make things worse, Erica was barely even looking at him; she only glanced between that flimsy ring and Stanley.

* * *

"Oh, I'm so happy for them. I know I don't know them that well, but how can you not be happy for a couple like that so obviously in love? They make such a cute couple too, don't they? I mean they look good together, they complement each other, they have so many things in common—both being in the movie industry and all. Even the things they don't have in common work for them. God, did you see the way he looks at her? Every woman wants to be looked at like that. Don't you think your friend found herself a good man?"

Brandon felt Jennifer's eyes burning into him, but it

was too much to ask of him to play along. Why didn't she just shut up anyway? Like she said, she didn't know either Erica or Stanley to be spending this chunk of her life yapping on about them.

"Brandon, are you okay? You don't seem happy about this at all."

"I just can't believe that guy. I mean, how tacky was that, using my restaurant location for a proposal? What a cheapskate. What a leech. What an unimaginative..."

"Brandon, come on. Not everyone can afford your luxuries—why shouldn't he seize the moment at a chance like that? It's not like he did it deliberately to spite you or disrespect you or anything."

"Yeah? Well, I feel pretty damned disrespected."

"I mean, I can sort of get that, but it still doesn't explain why you're this mad. And don't you dare deny it—it's all over you; I wish you could see yourself. You should be happy for her. Why are you so angry? Why does this whole thing bother you?"

"This is just too soon!"

He saw Jennifer frown out of the corner of his eye.

"Too soon? Sounds like they've known each other two or three years. You went to her graduation three years ago, didn't you? And she and Stanley met some months later? In what world is that too soon? Or is it just too soon for you? Is there something going on here I should know about? Do you have feelings for her?"

"Don't be silly, Jennifer—of course not; she's like a sister to me. What you've picked up on is the kind of resentment that comes from having to share something dear to you—the proprietary feelings family and best friends get. People feel this way about cars and video games—it's not that serious. I almost didn't want to take them to that restaurant 'cause I feel like it's kind of mine. So yeah, I guess feelings, but not like you're thinking. God, I saw her naked when she was four, for Christ's sake—when she ran out of the house giggling, and her mom ran out after her looking horrified." Brandon grinned at the memory. "My mom and I had been just about to go inside, but I took my clothes off and joined her 'cause she looked so happy. So free." He let out a breath and the silence stretched on for a few moments. "You're right," he said finally. "It feels too soon to me because I just found her again, and for a good chunk of our lives, I've looked after her, and now I can't do anything. She doesn't care what I think anymore."

Jennifer's sympathy was palpable. "I'm sure she does, Brandon—part of her probably still looks up to you. But she made the right decision for a part of her life you can't be involved in. There's a line somewhere, Brandon, and you're nearing it. Unless you know that her fiancé is some drug lord, ax murderer or philanderer with multiple venereal diseases, or that he beats women, children and puppies with crowbars, you need to back off." She paused. "This might seem a bit silly to you, but when I first saw her, I was a bit jealous. Of course, when I saw what a contented couple she and Stanley made, I realized I had gotten all worried for nothing. But you can't blame me, right? I mean, she's so pretty. Like, in a way you don't see every day or even once a week. Like Halle Berry with hazel eyes."

Brandon briefly looked at her. Was she insane? "She looks nothing like Halle Berry," he said.

"No, but I mean that type, you know? Like, Rihanna. Really, really pretty in a kind of exotic way."

Brandon shook his head, wondering what she was getting at. He decided he didn't have the patience to deal with it at the moment—his head was too full of other issues.

"Yes, she's really pretty, but you know what else? She's a nice person too. She's always been a good friend to me, kind and gentle. She used to actually love babysitting too—she loved kids. I always thought she'd be a kindergarten teacher or something because of the way she was; she'll probably be a great mom someday. Anyway, she'll need to toughen up out here, and I hope Stanley can help her with that."

Silence passed between them for a few moments. Then Jennifer said, "What did you and Erica talk about outside?"

"Similar to what we're talking about now, actually. I expressed my disapproval of Stanley and Erica chastised me for it. Of course, I reminded her I only had her best interests at heart, and she was all 'I'm not so sure about that.'" Brandon paused, realizing he didn't need to be too honest about it or go into too much detail. "I mean, he's too old for her, right? Look, I took this girl out to senior prom and when I went to pick her up at her house, before she came down, her dad chatted with me with a shotgun in his hand. I guess I get it now, you know? I just wanted Stanley to know not to fuck with her, not to hurt her. That's basically what I told her I was doing when she thought I was trying to ruffle Stanley."

"But you can see how much Stanley loves her, can't you? You should be relieved that she found someone who loves her like that."

"I just don't really know him! I don't know his ulterior motives or anything. He could be a great actor for all I know."

"But whose fault is that? You might have known more or had more influence if you had kept in contact with her, but you didn't."

Brandon felt stung. Then he said, "You're absolutely right."

"Of course I am. If she had sprung this on you while you guys were still close, maybe you would've had the right to feel the way you do, but the way I see it, this isn't your business anymore. She's a grown woman now—not some green teenager. I commend you for your concern, but again, clearly the couple is happy, and they're good for each other. And Erica has already made up her mind most importantly. Don't you realize? If you don't back off and respect her choices, you risk losing her again. Come down too hard and she'll back away, and all this reconciliation would be in vain." She put her hand over his and said softly, "She knows exactly what she's doing, Brandon. You have to trust her."

But despite her gentle, supporting words, and all the reason they seemed to be dipped in, as Jennifer yapped on and on, his mind kept churning, illness refusing to leave his stomach. His mouth was unable to force out one more smile.

Brandon nodded to everything Jennifer said, but no matter how soothing, encouraging or understanding her words were supposed to be, he could no longer process them. He couldn't get past the one thought that kept churning in his head, spreading and permeating his heart and every fiber of his being, getting louder and louder, vibrating and reverberating: *stop Stanley*.

PART II

STOP STANLEY

CHAPTER 6

BAIL

Brandon was determined to find a way to let Erica know that she was settling. How could she even think about binding herself to some old dude who just looked into cameras? Could he even go hiking with her? Did Erica even like hiking?

Either way, no matter what Erica or Jennifer said, he needed to step in. Marriage was a big deal—not something Erica should accept so lightly.

So what if she had been with the guy for a few years? That made it even worse, in his opinion—some forty-year-old dating a girl who had just turned legal a few years earlier.

Stanley was obviously a creep.

Brandon dialed Erica's number.

He couldn't believe how relieved he felt every time she actually picked up his call; he had no real reason to think that she wouldn't.

"Hey, bud—how about brunch?" he said when she

answered. "I want to hear how the auditions are going and everything."

"Thanks for the offer, Brandon, but I'd rather not; I'm pretty busy today."

"How about tomorrow? Come on, I know you have some time off between waitressing and auditions. Your days are pretty free."

"I'm not a waitress; I'm a promo model."

"What's that?"

"Advertising. Passing out freebies at events and stuff like that. And these jobs happen at all times of the day, Brandon."

"I hope you're not offended—most aspiring actors work restaurant gigs; I wasn't saying anything about you."

"I know, but you didn't even ask. I guess being presumptuous serves you well in business? Anyway, no to lunch or brunch or whatever this week—I'm really busy. Still sorting out lots of stuff. But thanks."

"Then when do I get to see you again? Let's not turn into those friends who live within twenty miles of each other and keep promising to meet up, but take two years to do it. This isn't the eighteenth century—it won't take a horse and a couple of weeks to travel. Come on, we can work around traffic."

She didn't respond.

Brandon let out a breath. "Look, I'm really sorry for the things I did and said to offend you, Erica. I want to make it up to you or at least apologize in person."

"I appreciate that, but I accept your apology over the phone. Look, I've got to go."

Brandon stared at his phone for a moment after she hung up and then regrouped.

He gave her a few days then tried again, but she eventually stopped responding to him altogether.

Well, she could ignore his calls and texts and invites to eat all she wanted, but there were some things she couldn't possibly ignore.

* * *

Brandon looked at the name on his caller I.D. and smiled. He knew his latest plan would work.

"Brandon! What the hell did you send me?"

Erica sounded like she was trying very hard not to shout at him.

"Great!" he said. "Everything arrived okay."

"No, no, no. Tell me why I'm looking at a pair of…I've never even heard of this brand, but these earrings look far too expensive. What is this?"

"Consider it a late birthday gift or graduation present. Or…I don't know—I'm-really-sorry-I-didn't-talk-to-you-for-three-years gift. Mostly the latter. Erica, I'm just trying to make it up to you. You're very valuable to me and the earrings don't reflect half that value."

"I don't even want to know how much this cost. I can't even guess."

"You don't have to and I won't tell you. I don't need you to feel guilty or tell me that you can't accept a gift like it or something silly like that. It barely made a dent in my account." *But it sure as hell's worth more than five times that ring your precious Stanley got.*

"Well, you're right. Doesn't matter what it's worth because regardless, I can't accept it."

"Don't be ridiculous. We're friends."

"Brandon, guy friends don't buy their female friends…what, six-figure priced earrings? Especially for no real reason. What's wrong with you? You haven't forgotten what it's like to be a normal person, have you? Do you realize how this looks to Stanley?"

"I'm not responsible for his insecurities. Obviously, that ring he got you could never compare, but why should anyone compare them? Why wouldn't he just see it for what it is? Are you really telling me I can't buy you anything?"

"He does see it for what it is, Brandon, that's the problem. He thinks you're swinging your dick around, so just stop. Pay attention to the girl you have."

But I don't want that girl, he almost said but stayed silent.

He heard Erica breathe out.

"Look, even if you and I know that there's nothing more to it, it looks bad. Think about it—what if some dude sends Jennifer some crazy expensive gift? You would seriously think, *innocent until proven not-so-innocent*? Please. And I know you said you don't really care about her—about anyone, apparently—but think about it objectively; consider it from the outside. I can't accept this gift, Brandon. Send someone to pick it back up and maybe give it to your girlfriend. She'll appreciate it—as long as you don't tell her you gave it to me first, that is."

***

A FEW DAYS LATER, when Jennifer came into the living room, Brandon was still smiling from his latest phone call.

He almost didn't notice her he was so distracted by his own cleverness. By the time Erica figured out what he had been up to, it would be too late and she would have unknowingly accepted his latest gift.

"What are you smiling about?" Jennifer asked, her mouth teased into a small grin.

"I just pulled off a big one," he said, and then remembered who he was talking to.

She looked at him expectantly.

Should he tell her?

Surely, she wouldn't make a big deal of it—as far as Jennifer was concerned, everything he did for Erica was because he was a caring, engaged friend.

"I pulled a few strings and did Erica a huge favor," he said.

"Oh? What kind of favor?"

"I got her a job!" he said. "Well, she'll get to meet with the director of some TV show, anyway. I passed her headshot on to a few folks I know, and she has a guaranteed part on an upcoming episode."

Jennifer's eyes widened. "Wow. That *is* a huge favor. Good for you. What are you hoping to get out of it?"

Brandon detected a change in atmosphere.

"I'm sorry?"

"Do you want her to see you as her savior? Do you

want her to feel indebted to you so that you can cash in later somehow? What is it?"

"What are you getting at, Jennifer?"

"Don't act like you don't know, Brandon. You know what you're doing, Erica knows what you're doing, and I know what you're doing. And I can't believe you think I'm so dumb or blind or whatever that you didn't think I'd catch on. Or else you're just that heartless and cruel to be throwing around how you feel about her like that."

She came close to him and he saw tears brimming in her eyes. "I never asked you for much, and I thought you were capable of at least giving me the basics: respect. And for a while, I think you gave that to me. But now that your 'friend' has come back, it's like you don't even care about me—like I could disappear and you wouldn't notice because you're too busy texting her or trying to send her gifts or working out big favors for her. I know that she hasn't asked you for any of it and that you just feel driven to do it, and that's how I know I've lost. If you felt about me anything close to how you feel about her, all this time and energy and cash you're putting into getting her to talk to you would be spent on me. But you don't feel that way about me. You never did, and you never will."

Brandon ignored his suddenly vibrating phone as he watched teardrops fall down Jennifer's face. Her voice was quiet and raw and it compelled him.

"At first I thought that's just how you were—that you didn't get deeply involved or crazy about anything—including people—besides your hobbies. You treated everyone the same as far as I could tell; in fact, what attracted you to me was that lightness about you. You didn't seem weighed down by anything, and I just figured that when one looks like you, and especially when one has easy access to everything like you do, that lightness is just what happens. You had this look in your eyes that said you were all about enjoying life; you were open to all parts of it and never took anything too seriously. You didn't seem to have yourself on any kind of pedestal despite all that you had going for you, and you even came after a girl like me—a normal girl. Still, you seemed to see the beauty in regular ol' me—you said you liked the richness of the chestnut of my hair, the way my eyes squashed when I smile." Her lips briefly turned up into a bitter, ghostly version of one. "You seemed to actually see me despite all the better-looking girls around."

She wiped her face. "But now I see that a passionate side to you *does* exist, and Erica seems to be the only one who can reach it. That look in your eyes when you talk about her..."

Brandon watched in horror as Jennifer deteriorated further into crying; in fact, she was practically blubbering, but she still managed to hold her sobs back enough to talk.

"Maybe it's not Erica's looks that has your attention now—you guys have a lot of history and I know that counts for something. For a lot. You two know each other probably better than anyone—family excluded, I'm guessing. You probably know all about each others' strengths and weaknesses, how to make each other laugh, how to comfort each other when a shoulder is needed."

She shook her head slowly. "I don't know what happened between you two back in the day—you never mentioned her to me before all of this—but it's clear that none of you got over it. Whatever tiff or falling out you guys had—it's become a shadow over us, and I know that it's not going anywhere till you guys resolve it. Everything would be all well and good if it was only that, but you guys haven't addressed the biggest elephant in the room here, the one that's never going away. Those glances between you—there's far more going on than you guys are letting on—even to yourselves, it seems. And I... I'm just not going to play second fiddle."

She wiped her face again. "I love you, Brandon, and I mean it. And I don't know when or if it'll ever go away, but there's no way I'm going to stay here and torture myself watching you guys make eyes at each other. She's clearly here to stay in your life, and I can't drive myself nuts over every touch, every glance, every meet-up for lunch. Every phone call, every text—I can't keep wondering: is this the time they'll finally admit how much they want each other?"

"You've got it so wrong, Jennifer."

Her expression turned knowing, sardonic.

"Do I? You should see the way your eyes light up when you talk to her or about her or when you think it's her calling you on the phone. You think I can't see through all your claims about feeling like a sibling to her? I mean, she's gorgeous, and I know some friends can look past that in their friends, but I don't believe it when it comes to you for a second because I've seen the way you *see* her. You look at her like a woman, not some girl friend."

She looked down, finally freeing him from her

accusatory, pain-filled eyes. "And I don't know what you've been dreaming about, but I've definitely heard you whisper her name in your sleep. And you can claim guilt gifts all you want, but buying her those expensive earrings you tried to pretend you bought for me—that was an obvious diss to Stanley; you're trying to show him up. I just can't be with a guy who does something like that; I admired you because you didn't throw your wealth around. You're not showing off with all kinds of fancy cars lined up along some gilded pathway in front of a mansion. I thought it might be because the money in your life was incidental, like your sense of self went beyond it, but it's clear that money makes you feel like someone, and if that's where your self-worth comes from, I want nothing to do with it."

She let out another breath. "You know, you really seemed like a nice guy, Brandon—a regular guy, anyway—but I see now that you're just another asshole. A self-absorbed, inconsiderate, shallow asshole. And no matter who you think you are, I deserve better."

Brandon didn't say another word.

He watched Jennifer leave the room, her words echoing in his head.

Even when she reemerged with her stuff packed, his mouth couldn't form words.

Before she left the house, she threw him one last sorrowful glance, and the open sorrow on her face finally dislodged the blockage in his throat.

"I'm sorry," he said gently, meaning every modicum of every syllable as he looked at her intently, knowing there was no going back from this moment and hoping that she at least believed the depth of regret he felt for hurting her.

Her face transformed in a way that told him she did.

"I'm keeping the earrings," she said softly. Then she left.

*** * * ***

Brandon had no idea how much time had passed when he finally decided to check his phone.

He saw a text message from Erica asking if he was available the next day for lunch.

Definitely, he texted back. *Anytime for you.*

He was glad she was finally responding again; she probably wanted to talk about the crazy audition she had where she ended up meeting the director.

He smiled at the thought.

Normally, he knew he would have filled with joy, but he was still a bit weighed down by the damage he had inflicted on Jennifer; he hated injuring an innocent bystander.

Then he remembered some of the things she said.

The worst part about what she flung at him was her conclusion that his money defined him after all.

What a bunch of crock—his money never defined him; it had nothing to do with how he was and never did. He was still the same guy now as he was before the jackpot, only with easier access to the best surfs and not having to think about the cost of anything. He could comfortably live the way he wanted to live and never even had a reason to throw his money around till now, in a desperate bid to keep Erica close to him.

He was sorry the impression Jennifer left with was so off-base and frustrated by her misinterpretation of his latest actions. Still, he was glad to be free to have his cake and eat it, too; after all, with Connor still flailing in the challenge, and Alec having long dropped out, no doubt he had already won the game and Alec's beach house was his.

Now, he could get the girl.

* * *

All heaviness left Brandon the next day once he started getting ready for his lunch date with Erica.

He had missed the presence of a body next to his overnight, but all he could think about was how much he wanted Erica to fill the new space.

He couldn't deny it to himself anymore—he wanted her, and not just as a friend to keep close or even just as a lover. He wanted her at his side and even wanted to see that stupid play she'd been in and hoped that there was a recording of it somewhere. He wanted Erica to look at him every day with those gorgeous doe eyes, and he wanted to fly her all over the world.

Heck, he even wanted to start making films again, some starring her.

He finally realized that his beef with Stanley had nothing to do with Stanley himself—Stanley was probably a nice guy and a loving partner, but so what? Brandon wanted Erica to himself in every way.

He couldn't wait to tell her.

He left home early and rushed to their agreed-upon location, arriving in record time.

He was grateful for the extra few minutes—he had time to run over what he planned to say to her in his mind.

As the meet-up time neared and he figured he had come up with the perfect words, he looked up to see someone approaching him, but it wasn't Erica.

Stanley was making his way over, and Brandon tried to look around him to see if Erica wasn't far behind.

Stanley sat opposite him.

"Expecting someone else?" he said.

"Yes, actually," Brandon said, trying to figure out what was going on. Then he realized what had happened.

"Ah! Looks like you figured out Erica isn't going to show up. Yes, it was me texting you."

"Does Erica know?"

"None of your business. Which is incidentally what I came here to tell you. Erica is my business, Brandon Wilde. She is going to be my wife shortly, and it would be best if you learned to respect our relationship now. In other words, in case it's having trouble getting through your water-logged brain, back off. Put your astoundingly selfish impulses aside and think about Erica for once."

He huffed before continuing. "I remember what it was like being your age. With or without money, you feel like the world can be yours for the taking, like you can do anything. Lucky for you, you don't have much more to conquer, hence why you've set your sights on Erica, I suppose—some reprieve from boredom. A new challenge.

"You know, after you disappeared from her life and she and I had started seeing each other, she mentioned you to me. She told me all about this old friend of hers who wouldn't talk to her anymore. You should have seen her face, Brandon—if I didn't love her by then, I certainly fell deeply for her in that moment seeing how hurt she was. The pain in her eyes—I knew I would always wonder about that girl and always hope and pray that she's happy and never runs into someone who could devastate her like that again. She is too gentle for it, too sweet to deserve the insensitivity of some thoughtless prick, so there was no way I was letting her back out there again when I knew I had it in me to take care of her and give her what she needed.

"In fact, you know what she said to me about you abandoning her? 'It was like my dad all over again. Someone you think is so necessarily bonded to you can walk away from you in an instant and never look back.' Her best friend in the world clearly didn't give a shit about her; she didn't think it could happen to her twice. But guess what? She blamed herself—figured she just wasn't lovable enough."

He paused to let out a breath. "Do you know how much work I had to do to convince her otherwise? You scarred her, Brandon. She is not some plaything or a tool you can use to prop yourself up for whatever selfish reason you have."

For the second time in two days, Brandon was left dumbstruck.

He sat there in the booth long after Stanley had gone, Stanley's words and the images of a younger, sadder Erica bombarding him.

It occurred to him that he really had been selfish when it came to everyone around him lately. He hurt Jennifer unnecessarily, he hurt Erica unnecessarily, and despite his gentle, but firm tone, he had hurt Stanley, too.

Brandon always had fun doing whatever he wanted to do, but he never meant to hurt anyone in the process and figured he never did until now.

Stanley was right—he needed to back off and do what was best for Erica.

Time to purge.

CHAPTER 7

MEN IN GRAY SUITS

Brandon knew what he had to do; he couldn't think of anything else to do—time to hit the surf. And not just any surf—he needed to leave California where the nearness of Erica would torture him until he ended up doing exactly what everyone had asked him to stop doing. He needed to put actual, appreciable distance between them, to cleanse himself and wash away all the negative energy surrounding and engulfing him. He needed to take some time off to do the best form of meditation he could imagine.

There was nothing like surfing to clear his head. Something about a coastline, the sudden remoteness of the signs of a city, the feel and sound of water, the mind focused on just one task as you got in the ocean made everything else drop away or feel less significant.

The only times other concerns filtered through out there was when he was exploring a new area and wasn't sure what kind of dangers could be lurking underneath the water between the corals and creatures. Still, surfing was the most soothing activity he could fathom, and it hadn't yet failed in taking him to a place of zen.

And who said he never took a risk? He took all kinds of risks out there in various oceans all around the world—from Hawaii to New Zealand to South Africa.

Brandon thought hard about where to go this time. Not Indonesia and not Tahiti—somewhere he hadn't gone before, perhaps.

Then it came to him: Australia—especially this time of year.

He considered a specific part of Australia he had avoided—an area off Tasmania—and then figured that now was as good a time as any to conquer it.

* * *

Brandon called up a few of his buddies to accompany him.

One couldn't make it due to work obligations and unnecessarily threw in his face the reminder that not everyone could just take off whenever they wanted.

The other was down for the weekend trip since Brandon was paying for it—his friend, Pete, had no girl at the moment and didn't work on weekends, so he was always down for a free ride.

But once they arrived at the beach, Pete seemed to suddenly change his mind, his footsteps slowing.

Brandon looked at him, disrupted by the change of pace.

All Pete said was, "Something doesn't feel right, man."

Brandon looked at him like he had lost his mind.

"Are you kidding me? The weather feels great, and look at that wave we just missed," he said, pointing. "It's not perfect out here, but I'm about to have an amazing time, regardless."

"Well, go on without me. I'll wait it out here for a bit," Pete said as he sat on the sand. "It could've been something I ate or something, but I actually feel kind of ill."

"You're a fucking wuss, Pete," Brandon said, chuckling. "I mean, look—even dolphins are about." He pointed at the animals jumping between the waves, seeming to have a grand time.

"They had an attack out here just two weeks ago, you know," Pete said, looking at him gravely.

Brandon waved him off.

"Locals are always trying to make stuff sound more exciting than it is. Remember when we went scuba diving in the Bahamas and the locals kept talking about some kind of *sharktopus* in the blue holes?"

"Yeah, but *sharktopus* is obviously not real. Sharks are."

Brandon ignored him and headed out.

* * *

FOR THE FIRST time in his life, Brandon found his concentration broken by something from the outside, from his life on land.

His mind kept going to Erica, and he was determined to get to the point where his mind was clear and he could just focus on the waves.

But try as he might, he couldn't stop thinking about how much he missed her and how much he longed to see her face again. He wanted nothing more than for her to be out here with him—where Pete was, watching. He wanted her to see just how good he was. He wanted to teach her the basics and watch her splash around for a bit. Maybe she'd be a natural.

He wondered what she looked like in a bikini, and tried hard not to think about Stanley getting to see all of her, in and out of a swimsuit.

He didn't know how long he had been out in the ocean, and it took him a while to register a shout from the beach, but only about a second to realize what the shout was about.

He turned and saw the shadow of a creature no one wanted to see out here—especially on a flimsy board dwarfed in comparison to the giant creature near it.

His heart dropped, but he knew he had to stay calm and just try to head back.

But all of that went out of the window when he found himself suddenly lifted into the air, and he watched his board get clamped between several rows of teeth—only part of the shadowy nightmare he had glimpsed earlier—before he tumbled into the water.

Brandon immediately put his swimming skills to work.

When he felt something brush against his leg, he moved faster, trying to keep his movements smooth.

Please don't let this be the last thought I have of Erica, he thought right before he felt a strange sensation in one of his legs. It felt like a burn at first, and then a razor-sharp pain raced through his limb.

He kept moving forward, and when he saw what looked like blood darkening the water, he was prepared to turn and try to punch the large creature in the nose or the gills, to jab it in the eyes, but after a moment, he felt the shark let go of his leg.

Brandon continued making his way to shore, hoping the beast didn't change its mind and come after him again for another taste test, while hoping his leg was still attached to him and didn't just feel like it was, like he'd heard happened with amputees.

He noticed Pete coming toward him then felt himself pulled in the rest of the way to shore.

He became aware of lying on the sand and of Pete over him, using his shirt to make a sort of tourniquet for his injured leg and yelling for help, before eventually blacking out.

* * *

"FUCKING HELL, Brandon, you scared the bejeezus out of me," a blurry Alec said, looking down at him, his blue eyes intense with concern.

Brandon wondered why his brother was in his bedroom. Then he looked around and realized he wasn't lying in his own bed after all; instead, he was in what looked like a hospital room.

"Alec, what're you doing here? What is this?"

"You mean you don't remember the shark that took a bite out of you? Anyway, Pete called me and I came right away. Man, you're a lucky bastard, as usual. Your orthopedic surgeon said you'll make a speedy recovery—no nerve, bone, or artery damage or anything. But if the bite had been just two centimeters closer..." Alec made a slashing motion across his neck. "You're lucky Pete has half a brain—that tourniquet helped, and he got help for you pretty quickly; an ambulance was at the location in no time. You're in Gold Coast Hospital, and we've got the best people working on you, brother." Alec patted his face. "You won't be here long, and you'll be surfing in shark-infested waters again in no time."

Alec's words started fading away as Brandon found himself irresistibly pulled into unconsciousness again. The last thing he heard his brother say before he blacked out once more was, "By the way, who's Erica?"

CHAPTER 8

PICKING UP CUES

"Um, Erica?"

Erica double-checked the name on her screen. The call said Brandon, but the voice—although male—was unfamiliar.

"Yes?" she said uncertainly.

"This is Alec, Brandon's brother. My brother's out cold right now, but he has said your name more than once, so I figure you're someone he would call if he could."

Erica's heart sped up. "What are you talking about?" she asked.

"My brother's out from pain meds. He had an incident off Tasmania. Great white attack."

"Wait, what?"

"We're in Australia. If you know my brother, you know why he was here. The shark took a bite out of his board and managed to clamp down on his leg. He got lucky, I guess, since he's still here. Anyway, just thought

I'd let you know in case you were expecting to hear from him or anything."

Erica stared at the phone, her mouth wide open long after Alec hung up. She didn't know how long she sat there, feeling stuck between a dream and a nightmare.

That call couldn't have been real, could it? She nearly lost Brandon, just like that?

And what was she supposed to do now—just wait until he got back to California? When was that supposed to be? How badly was he hurt? Did he still have all of his limbs? Was he completely out of the woods?

"Erica Cain, you're up," the casting assistant suddenly said.

Erica knew there was no way she could do her audition now and wished she hadn't forgotten to turn off her phone. Then again, she would have missed such a hugely important call.

She was about to leave but remembered that the scene she'd been about to read for was an emotional one.

She was in exactly the right place to hit this audition out of the park.

The only problem was, once she started crying, whether or not she'd be able to stop.

* * *

Erica didn't realize she was pacing until Stanley called her out on it.

"I know you're nervous about your friend and all, but his brother said he'll be okay, didn't he? He'll be back in a few weeks or so, right?"

"Yes, but what if something goes wrong and I'm not there?"

"Sounds like he got pretty lucky and he'll recover just fine."

"I just..." Erica couldn't stop wringing her hands. She couldn't remember the last time she did that. "He could have died!" she said at last. "The shark could have dragged him out and tore him to pieces, or he could have bled out from the wound. He would have been all the way over there and I..." Erica covered her face with her hands and took a few deep breaths, shaking her head.

Ever since that call, she kept playing out several nightmarish scenarios in her head. She would have never been able to forgive herself if Brandon had died out there, after she had given up so many chances to take him up on an offer to lunch or whatever stupid excuse he came up with to try to see her.

She couldn't fathom never being able to look into his face again, and even though she had been assured he'd be almost back to normal in a few weeks, the fact that she couldn't just drive over to see him was killing her.

Why couldn't they just fly him to California for the rest of his recovery? Was he just choosing to stay there?

She knew her emotions had gotten the better of her, but she was powerless to stop her irrational thoughts.

She didn't realize Stanley had been making his way over to her until he reached her and put his arms around her.

She snuggled into his hug.

***

Erica saw Brandon's name pop up on her screen and she grabbed her cell, answering immediately.

"Brandon, are you okay?"

"Yes, Erica. Just calling to let you know all went well and I'm back in California. Sorry Alec worried you like that, but I'm fine now—good as new. Anyway, like I said, I was just calling to let you know everything's back to normal; don't worry—I won't bother you again."

"Just hold a second! It's still a big deal and I want to see you! I want to see for myself."

"You don't have to. Here, I'll text you a pic..."

"Don't play with me, Brandon. When can I see you? You have no idea..." She stopped, reconsidering what she had been about to say. "You have no idea how much worrying I've been doing." *How many nights I couldn't sleep thinking about you. How many auditions I tanked because I couldn't get my mind right.* "I even had a nightmare one night about some giant shark dragging you out to sea." *And that I would never see you again. I woke up crying, Brandon—inconsolable. Blubbering, I tell you!*

Erica took a moment to gather herself, hearing a dangerous break in her voice at her last sentence. Her emotions were about to overwhelm her again—the relief from hearing Brandon's voice at last was too much for her.

"Well, I'm glad you still care, Erica."

"Don't be ridiculous, Brandon—I've never stopped. You're my friend. Now direct me where to go!"

* * *

"Fucking pit-bulls of the sea is what they are," Brandon said as they sat on his couch while Erica examined the scar on his thigh.

She looked up at him. "Was that some kind of suicide mission? I've only heard bad things about Australian waters, usually involving great white sharks. What possessed you to go there?"

"There's always a risk when it comes to surfing, Erica. And it's not like people are getting attacked left and right every single day. Contrary to popular belief, shark attacks are not exactly common; you watch too much Shark Week."

"Yeah, well, some places are riskier than others. God, I can't believe I almost lost you!" she said, sitting up completely and drinking him in with her eyes again.

Seeing him after just eight weeks impacted her even greater than when she finally saw him again after three years. No doubt it was because she knew she had almost lost him forever and had been tortured by the knowledge of how close he had actually come to death.

God, how she missed that beautiful face of his and those sparkling eyes. That slight dimple in his cheek when he smiled. The familiarity of his tall, muscled frame. That voice capable of dipping into a goose-bump-inducing rumble...

"I can't believe I was that close to not seeing you again too," he said, the dreaded rumble making an appearance, and his eyes locking on hers in the way that rendered her helpless.

His blue depths smoldered.

The intensity of his gaze silenced her completely, and all she could do was wait for him to move toward her, and then accept him when his arms came around her, and she was suddenly near enough to sense his pounding heart. Then she raised her head slightly in anticipation of his kiss, and with one of his hands cupping the back of her head to hold her in place, he delivered the kiss, and it was no gentle kiss.

Erica got the distinct impression that Brandon was not about to take his time as wild need emanated from him.

"Erica, I want you," he said, breaking the kiss. Then he kissed her again hungrily.

When his lips left hers again, they moved to her neck and a tingling sensation made its way through her entire body.

She knew that she was ready for him, and whether he was about to take his time or not, she didn't care—she wanted him now.

He lifted her up and took her to his bedroom where his lips continued to meet various parts of her body, each touch sending a jolt through her, and she was soon near the point where she needed him to go faster—to rip all their clothes off and just take her, easing the tingling between her legs and quenching her desire to have him fill her. Ten years had been far too long to wait for this.

"I want to taste all of you, Erica," he said, and she had no protest to offer. She couldn't think, couldn't form words, couldn't do anything but breathe deeply with her heart having sped up the way it had.

Brandon took her top off and flung it aside almost violently.

His own shirt came off, and as many times as she had seen him shirtless in photos and even in person, it did not prepare her for the hard, tanned body over her now, looking every bit like some sun-kissed god.

Then he suddenly stopped his frantic movements and something in his face changed.

She knew what he was thinking, and she couldn't let him. There was no way she was letting him stop and apologize; this moment had to happen.

"Take me, Brandon," she said. "Please don't stop."

He looked relieved as he continued raining kisses down on her while removing the rest of their clothes.

"You have no idea," he said between kisses, "how much I want you."

"Yes, I do," she said, looking at him directly.

When his fingers touched her wet spot, she nearly exploded right then. The sensation was too much—everything was heightened to the point that everything he did to her had her on edge.

"God, Brandon, please…"

He finally gave her what she wanted as she felt him fill her with his thick, stiff organ, and even her wildest dreams and fantasies weren't half as good as the real thing.

Erica's heart kept swelling with joy and love, and every time she thought it would explode, it only seemed to expand more.

She had forgotten what true happiness felt like. She had felt flashes of it on stage, at the news of booking a new job, and even with Stanley, but compared to what she felt now, those particular moments suddenly seemed more ordinary. If those had been moments of happiness and joy, what she felt now was the very definition of ecstasy and euphoria.

"I love you," she said as she snuggled up to him once they had exploded together and collapsed, pulsating against each other.

His breath seemed to catch, but when she looked at him, his eyes were closed as if he was sound asleep.

She let herself drift off with him, smiling, an arm wrapped around him.

* * *

"I couldn't have awakened to a better sight," Brandon said when he finally awoke.

Erica had been watching him since awakening just a few minutes earlier herself.

"Is it really you, Erica?" He reached out and touched her hair. "Wow, you're an angel." The contact of his fingers on her scalp made her all tingly again. He seemed to be enjoying passing his fingers gently through her curls. "I've wanted to touch you like this for a while," he said in a low voice. "And now we're here, and you're so soft and smooth and beautiful and everything I imagined." He put his face next to hers and sniffed.

She giggled. "Okay, weirdo."

"I love your smell," he said. "I'm imprinting it on my brain for the days I can't see you; in fact, I won't wash these sheets for a while."

Just as the thought occurred to her, he said, "Don't worry, everything has been laundered since Jennifer left. We have a fresh start." His hand cupped her face in a way that forced her to look at him. "What do we do now, Erica?"

"So you and Jennifer are no longer together?" she asked. He nodded. "But I'm still with Stanley."

The lightness in his manner disappeared as he looked at her intently. "I want you, Erica."

Erica's heart sped up again. She had waited for those words for so long and yet...

"Um, let me think for a sec."

About what? she asked herself. This was what she wanted, what she had always wanted. So what was the problem?

You know. He wants you for now. This is exactly what you've been running away from. He's not going to hang around, and it won't be long before he's on to the next thing. And he'll probably stop speaking to you in the meantime.

"I have to really think about this," she said, getting up and looking for her clothes.

"What is there to think about?" he asked, looking genuinely confused. "We both want the same thing."

"Do we? Because I'm not just here for a ride."

"Erica, I wouldn't treat you like that..."

"You didn't set a good precedent; I have no reason to believe you. I mean, do you even love me?"

"Of course I do, Erica."

"No, I mean...you know what I mean."

"Yes!" he said, looking so sincere that she almost

believed him. "You were the only thing I could think about out there when I thought I was going to die!"

"And if you hadn't been about to die, you wouldn't have thought about me at all, right?"

"This is just silly, Erica. I'm here now, and my eyes have been opened. And yes, damn it, it took a lot to get there, but I did—I realize I should be with you."

"For me or for you?"

"Excuse me?"

"Do you need to be with me to fulfill your own needs or to fulfill mine?"

The confusion on his face said all she needed to hear. If he didn't understand what she was asking, he didn't understand what she needed from him and why she couldn't just risk it all and throw everything away with Stanley to be with him.

Brandon did not have the capacity for depth unless it involved the ocean.

Things tended to work out for him when it came to chance, but not so much for her.

CHAPTER 9

IMPACT ZONE

Brandon didn't understand what had happened.

After such a beautiful moment and the emotionally harrowing time they'd both obviously had over the past several weeks, what was Erica doing?

She said she needed to think, give her some time to think, he thought. *Don't push yet. Call her tomorrow.*

When the next day came, he dialed Erica's number.

Surely she had come to her senses by now.

When she answered, she said, "Brandon, I don't mind you calling every now and then. I was wrong to ignore you as much as I did before...you know, the attack, so I definitely want to keep you in my life, but as a friend."

Brandon felt his brows furrowing.

"Erica, I don't get it—we fit so well together..."

"For just a moment, Brandon, but as a real couple, it can't work. We have nothing in common."

"Yes, we do, and yesterday demonstrated quite a few things we have in common—the way you react when your lips touch my body..."

"You know what I mean! I'm not talking about sex here, I mean real things. Things that sustain a relationship."

"What the hell else do you think we need in common to work?"

"Anything! Interests, taste in movies..."

"We both have white mothers. How's that?"

He heard her let out a breath.

"Come on, Erica, we grew up together! We're from the same neighborhood. We didn't go to any of the same schools, but we know each other's personalities in and out and still like each other! We have long grown to accept the flaws between us. Christ, the way you seem to look at it, my dating options should be limited to tall, billionaire surfer chicks. What the hell kind of odds is that?"

"Wait, you're a billionaire?"

"Assets combined with Connor's, yes—he and I count our shit together. Anyway, you see where I'm going? What you're saying right now just sounds like an excuse—it doesn't make sense at all. I don't expect to have a ton of things in common with the girl I'm with—I expect to be able to count that stuff on one hand. What I'm looking for is not someone who's the female equivalent of me; I'm looking for someone I can have a good time with. That I actually *want* to spend my time with."

"Could've fooled me. I'm surprised this stuff is even happening between us considering I'm not your type."

"Now what does that mean?"

"Come on—I remember Tara and the other girls you dated. Even if they didn't have that much in common with you, they sure had a lot in common with each other: athletic, Barbie types."

"You're crazy—the one after Tara was no Barbie."

"But she did look like Jennifer. It's the first thing I thought when I saw Jennifer."

"I don't even know what you're trying to say with all of this. Clearly, I don't just date blondes or brunettes. I go where my heart goes, and right now, it's pointing at you."

"Nice. Believable even—if it wasn't for what just happened with the girl you were with recently. You know—the one you used for some stupid challenge?" She exhaled deeply. "Look, Brandon, I've always been a supporting character in your life and I don't think that's going to change. You're always just surfing. Not away from or toward anything, just surfing."

"I'm gonna need you to clarify."

"Everything about you is based on luck and that's the opposite of stability to me. You don't work for anything—everything just falls into your lap. Well, not when it comes to me, it won't."

"You have a short-term memory—you've fallen into my lap more than once."

Brandon got the distinct impression that, had they been in person, Erica would have slapped him silly.

"I'm going to ignore that," she said. "Look, feel free to call and keep me updated with the usual mundane things friends talk about. I do love you as a friend, Brandon, and I don't want to lose you again."

When Erica hung up, Brandon's emotions were tied

up in knots. He was angry, hurt, and felt resentful of all that talk about luck; he always hated it when someone brought it up. Alec used to get on his nerves talking about it, and even though Brandon could see where everyone was coming from, he felt belittled nonetheless.

"You guys are fucking charmed," Alec had said to him once.

"What are you talking about?" Brandon asked him.

"So, first of all, you're the first set of twins in the family out of nowhere, right? And then—god, too many incidents from your childhood to go over right now. Do you know you missed getting hit by a car by like an inch when you were two? And now you guys hit that jackpot..."

But that was just life, wasn't it? Some people had to work hard for all they got while others got the same things handed to them.

Besides, Alec was lucky in several ways himself. All through school, he tended to understand lessons easier, faster. If Brandon had cared enough, he would have had to work extremely hard to get even close to the same result. Alec didn't have to work his brain for an A, but Brandon had to put in effort to get C's and Bs.

Brandon let out a heavy breath.

Everyone had their own kind of luck, didn't they? Some people were born with a better hairline than others, some grew up with two sane parents, some people got jobs right out of high school, and some people had to work hard to gain or lose five pounds.

The worst part was that most people seemed

oblivious to their own special luck, too distracted by the luck of others.

He had even heard Tara say that she wished her hair was thicker, and he had wondered at a girl like her nursing some perceived flaw.

It seemed everyone wished they had something that someone else had, and no one was happy.

Still, despite not liking when others pointed it out, Brandon knew exactly how lucky he was.

But where the hell was his special luck now?

* * *

Brandon waited a few more days then called Erica again.

"Are you back with Stanley?" he asked when she picked up.

He heard her sigh. "Yes."

"Have you slept with him since...?"

"How the hell's that your business all of a sudden?"

"Well, it is. I feel like you're kind of mine now."

"Well, I'm not, because what we did was a mistake."

"How can you call what we did 'a mistake?' 'Inevitable' is what I think you meant to say, Erica; we've had feelings between us for almost a decade and they were always kind of one-sided until recently. I may not have seen how amazing you were then, but I sure as hell see it now."

"I don't know what you want me to do about that. I have a man—I have Stanley. And he doesn't just have feelings for me, he loves me."

"But I love you too, Erica! "How the hell can you go back to him after we...?"

"I told him about it, so he knows. I felt way too guilty and he deserved to know what we did. It's never a good idea starting a relationship with some secret hanging over you."

"So let me get this straight—our making love was okay with him?"

Erica didn't answer right away; in fact, it seemed to him that her breathing had sped up.

Then she said, "He told me that once he saw you, he knew we had to get it out of our system considering our history."

"What the hell's that supposed to mean? And did you? Am I out of your system? Because something tells me I'm not, Erica—that I'm probably lodged deeper now. You can't go back to him, not after what we've done." Then he paused. Though he dreaded the answer, he had to know. "So have you been with him since or not?"

"None of your business! Look, I'm with him, and that's that. He wants to be with me."

"*I* want to be with you, Erica."

"Great. For how long? Is this a twist for your latest dare with your brothers? What is it this time, Brandon? Biracial babes?"

"I would never do that to you, I told you that."

"Yeah, well, I don't know that. I was there when you treated me with the kind of disregard it would take, so why should I believe you now?"

"Come on, you've been around me practically my whole life. I treasure you tremendously. I fucked up letting us drift before, but I would never turn you into a plaything."

"And what else?"

"What do you mean?"

He heard her let out another frustrated breath. "You still don't get it. Just leave me alone, Brandon. We'll always be good friends, don't you worry; I'm still partially yours. We'll just be careful from now on and I won't let myself get in a situation like the other day with you again. But we'll still talk about everything like good old buddies. From a distance. Over the phone here and there—none of the meeting up stuff."

"Why? Because you're afraid of what I'll do to you once you get around me again? Afraid of having your feathers ruffled? Not sure you can handle it if we get close to each other? Are you afraid I'll have you naked and beneath me, begging me to take you..."

"Fuck you, Brandon. So what? Yeah, my body reacts to you, big deal. It doesn't matter in the long run—we both want different things out of life. Opposite things, in fact. I told you, I want stability..."

"Says the woman pursuing acting as a career."

"At least I've chosen something! And everything I've done is toward that goal."

"And that's why you picked Stanley, right? Because of his skill set and the potential connections, I'm guessing?"

"Fucking hell, Brandon, you're an asshole. In that case, why don't I just take you up on what you're offering me? You can buy my way into a film, right? PR, classes with the best in the biz—your money will handle all of that, right? You must know some people who know prominent directors—why am I still saying no to all of that?"

"Because you're a fool, Erica—I am clearly all you need."

"Wow. You're the fool, Brandon—an arrogant one. Let's see how much longer it takes for you to realize that. In the meantime, and for the rest of time, don't bother me with this nonsense about us being together again."

PART III

CUTBACK

CHAPTER 10

SURF'S UP

There were few times in his life Brandon felt like he had been pushed onto the ice of some skating rink and all he could do was flail and flop around, and then fall over and over again, despite wearing the proper gear. He had felt that way with Tara when nothing he could do was enough to keep her, and he felt that way now. Except this time, it felt worse—less desperation, more despair.

He couldn't lose Erica again—not now, not ever.

Brandon remembered Alec mentioning some place in Napa, and he got a strong impression then that his brother was planning to finally put down roots.

He knew what was coming once Alec put his Hawaiian beach house up as the prize for their latest challenge; it all seemed symbolic.

He remembered wondering if, two years from now, at Alec's current age, he would end up like his brother and suddenly want to settle.

Now here he was, wanting what Alec had already.

Brandon had rarely felt envious before—not even when Alec made his first million. Brandon had silently applauded his brother for keeping his nose to the grindstone and felt happy for him that his hard work had paid off, but he had never coveted his money or the things his brother's new money could buy.

Until that Hawaiian beach house.

The minute Alec flew them all to Hawaii to check it out and he laid his eyes on the beautiful structure in prime position for beaches and surfing, he wanted it. Now, it was finally his, and still he wanted more.

Brandon suddenly realized how Alec could part with the house, seemingly with no regrets. He understood fully how a home could depend on something more than just a beautiful structure in a prime location. Alec's home was wherever he could settle with Dahlia, and if she wanted to live in Napa, Italy or Timbuktu, Alec would take her there, happily settling wherever she chose.

Brandon felt compelled to dial his brother's number.

"Hey," Alec answered, and Brandon wasn't sure what he wanted to say exactly, so he stayed silent for a few more moments as he gathered his thoughts.

"Is this about Erica?" Alec asked. "That *is* you, isn't it, Brandon?"

"Yes, I'm here. And yes, it's about Erica. Alec, how did you convince Dahlia to be with you?"

"Wow, this *is* serious. To tell you the truth, getting her to date me wasn't so hard—it was getting her to stay with me after your brother got to her; I almost lost her."

Uh oh.

Brandon knew what he was about to hear wouldn't be good; Alec only verbally disowned Connor in such a way after Connor had done something despicable.

Your brother broke my iPad!

Your brother downloaded a virus and made me lose my work!

Your brother caused me a million in damages letting those hooligans in my house!

Your brother blabbed about you guys winning the lotto and it got around to Tara. Why do you think she suddenly came back to you?

"What did he do?" Brandon said, feeling ill.

"He basically told Dahlia I was just with her for the challenge, and then called her a piece of shit—although not exactly in those words, but essentially. He told her she wasn't worthy of our pedigree, and that the only way I could be with her was for some dare. The worst part was that he knew that wasn't true—he knew how much I loved her. Needless to say, he and I are no longer on speaking terms."

Alec let out a breath. "He obviously hasn't told you anything about this. Figures. Probably thought it'd all blow over, so why bother? Anyway, I didn't give up on Dahlia; there's no way I could, the way I feel about her. I've never wanted anything more in my entire life, so I kept at her till she gave me another shot and could risk believing in me again. So I guess, as with anything you really want that won't just fall into your lap, full steam ahead, brother. I didn't lose her in the end, but fuck Connor."

Brandon opened his mouth to protest and then closed

it. Alec had a right to feel the way he did. Besides, he was clearly still angry.

"When did this happen?"

"A few months ago."

"I'm sorry. Connor's such an ass sometimes."

"Yeah well, he's definitely not invited to the wedding. Don't you dare pass on the details to him either."

"Not a risk when I don't have them."

"You will, soon; Dahlia's still sorting everything out. Anyway, good luck with Erica, man. Sounds like you really love her—in which case, you don't really need my advice. Go get her."

But all of a sudden, Brandon felt compelled to call his brother, Connor, instead.

* * *

"Connor, what the hell?" Brandon said when he answered. "Why did you try to ruin Alec's relationship?"

"Old news. They're still together, aren't they? I didn't do shit."

"That's not the point. You almost did. What kind of asshole move was that? What got into you?"

"She had a right to know what the deal was. I've been trying this new thing about being honest and upfront."

"I don't believe that for a second. What's really going on with you?"

"Why are you acting so concerned all of a sudden?"

"I'm always concerned about you—you're my brother."

"Whatever. Look, if you just called to give me a

talking to about Alec, stuff it. Keep your own affairs in order—romantically, anyway, since I'm the one who has to clean up your financial messes."

"Whoa. Didn't know you resented your role keeping an eye on things. Besides, when have I ever been financially irresponsible? You're acting like I've been spending like crazy."

Brandon was no fool—while he had squirreled away enough money to cushion himself should anything happen, he also knew that he had one life, and all that money they had—what use was it if it just sat somewhere, growing? "I have two fun cars, a place in Santa Barbara and a place in Newport Beach. That's it. I get good deals when I travel. Hell, the most expensive thing I've bought in a while was a gift for Erica."

"Who Erica?"

"You know—the one from back when we were kids."

"You guys are together now?"

"I'm working on it. And don't try to fuck with us."

"Sounds like you're doing a good job of it all by yourself. Why are you having such a hard time? That never happens. Well, except for Tara, I guess—she's the only one able to resist your charms so far."

"You really don't care who you hurt, Connor?"

"Yeah, like I'm the one stringing along an old friend. You decided to keep the challenge going, it seems?"

"She's not a part of any of that shit, and I'm not planning to string her along; I love her."

"So let me get this straight: if I fuck with you guys, you'll disown me too." He paused for a few moments, and when his voice came, the quality of it had changed, mellowing out. "Man, you should have seen the look in Alec's eyes—I've never seen him so furious. And what the hell, for some girl?"

"If this was a few months earlier, I'd probably be where you are, but I understand Alec on this one completely."

"Do these girls have magical vaginas? You guys would just cut me off like that, your own flesh and blood? Especially you, womb-mate?"

"You've never loved a girl like this so you don't get it, but one day, maybe you will. Yeah, I've spent a large part of my life with you, sharing everything, and of course you mean the world to me. But it's just a different thing when it comes to Erica. No, wait—same thing, different form. I can't imagine being content with just spotty conversations with you and Alec here and there and splashing around in water my whole life. There's no way the three of us are going to end up living together and sharing our daily lives like we were kids, maintaining that level of companionship into our old age. You're my brothers and I love you, and my life would be incomplete without you too. I just want Erica to be on my sidelines with you guys, but more than that—I need her with me every step of the way, whatever I end up doing. I want to watch from her sidelines too; I need that closeness, that intimacy, and I thought I was okay with just a semblance of it from time to time, but I'm not."

Brandon suddenly felt like a veil had been lifted. His love and need for Erica had never been clearer. He wanted her in his life permanently, needed her there when he got home from whatever—surfing, board meeting. He wanted to hear all about her auditions and when she booked jobs, what her day was like on set, about her fellow actors, troubles with getting in the zone or whatever it was that actors did. He wanted to see her smile every day, watch her eyes light up when they settled on him, hold her against him, kiss her fears and frustrations away. He wanted her warm body next to his every single night for the rest of their lives.

"Wow. Guess you're really into her, huh?"

"I can't imagine my life without her, Connor—literally. I'm glad you and I are still close and I hope we remain that way our entire lives, but you can't give me what she can."

"Yeah, I guess babies and shit. So what's happening? Why can't you just tell her this? Does she not love you? 'Cause I'd find that hard to believe—she made goo-goo eyes at you a lot. But I guess she could have grown out of it."

"No, she loves me—I know it. She just doesn't trust me. She thinks I'm not serious and that I'll end up playing with her heart or something. She doesn't believe in my love for her, and I guess I can see why she wouldn't considering...well, everything. Look, I'm having a hard time reaching her and I don't want to seem too stalker-y and have her boyfriend come after me. Not that I can't take him—but I don't want to give her a reason to resent me and push me further away, you know? I just don't know the right balance of assertiveness in this case; I don't know how much pressure to apply."

"I hear you, bro. Don't give up."

* * *

Brandon was surprised to see Connor's name pop up on his screen the next day. Although emotionally close, he and his twin were nowhere near speaking to each other daily—a few times a month was more like it.

Brandon answered warily.

"I've been a bit bored lately, so I decided to help you with this Erica thing," Connor began, and Brandon's heart sank.

"Fuck, Connor. What did you do?"

"No, don't worry. I wanted to do for you the opposite of what I did to Alec. I know you said not to get in the way and all that, but you won't be mad, I promise. So I called her and she picked up—good thing she doesn't have my number, right? Or she might have ignored me too. But she picked up and I told her what you told me. The good news is, she didn't hang up right away once I pleaded your case and she found out who I was. The bad news is, I found out she's getting married soon."

"Oh, I know that; I was there when they got engaged."

"No, I mean, like, really soon. She said just forget it—the decision had already been made, blah blah blah, and that she and...Stanley, I think? They're getting married in two days."

Brandon shot up.

"Two days? Are you pulling my leg?"

"Nope. Your girl's about to marry someone else really soon, Brandon—unless she was straight up lying. Which Erica sucks at if I recall correctly. So anyway, I guess that's the only bad part. The bright side is, you can probably still stop it. She said they're going to the county clerk in Beverly Hills bright and early to pick up and pay for their marriage license—she already sent in the application. Now, that's a lot of detail if you ask me. Something tells me she wants you to stop it." He paused. "Good luck, bro," he said. "And I love you too."

CHAPTER 11

THE SHOW MUST GO ON

I'm doing the right thing. I'm doing the right thing.

Erica kept reminding herself every time a doubt crept in or she looked at Stanley that the two of them had come to the best conclusion: get the legal part of their marriage out of the way and then just throw a big party later on. The most important thing was that they make everything official and become husband and wife sooner than later.

A friend of hers had done the same thing and had no regrets.

"Who knows how long we would have been waiting for all the funds just to get married?" her friend had said. "Who cares when the real thing happened anyway? Just make a big deal about it to everyone later when you can afford it. You don't even have to tell anyone you're already legally married."

Erica decided she and Stanley would do the same

and they made a promise to each other not to tell a single soul.

Erica felt horrible about not having her mother there, and she had to convince herself that although this was the real thing, it really wasn't, considering no one was there to share it. Her mother wouldn't actually be missing anything when it came down to it—what she didn't know wouldn't hurt her, like everyone else. Later on, they would treat the wedding ceremony like they were actually doing it for the first time.

And Stanley looked so happy about their decision, how could she not be happy too, even though it had all been his idea to begin with?

Besides, she needed to prove her devotion to him. After seeing his face—the disappointment and anguish on it once she made her confession about her evening with Brandon—she would have done anything for him, given in to any request.

He had her worried for a while when he spent some time locked up in their room alone once she broke the news.

She realized then how much she had almost thrown away.

Stanley was her rock—what would she do all by herself in this city without him? His presence and support meant more to her than she'd realized.

When he came out of the room, his face was red, and she figured he had spent some time crying, which made her feel even worse.

Then he said, "Can I talk to you?" and when she nodded, he led her to the couch where they sat down.

"Although I can't say I'm surprised it happened, it hurts like hell, Erica—I can't tell you how much. But I still love you. I know you guys have a history, and the way I saw him look at you the night of our double date, I knew we had a problem. Especially with what I know of how things ended between you. One great thing about being my age is being able to put things in perspective. I've had a lot of experience, and I knew in my gut you guys had to take care of that unspoken unfinished business between you; the energy between you two was palpable. You're both young and still exploring all sorts of issues. Most of all, despite this mistake, I know your heart, Erica, and I know you love me. I know we'll make a great couple and I'm still glad I'm going to marry you. We'll make a great team. I will do all I can to support you and be there for you. I will love you to my grave, Erica."

By then Erica was crying, filled with gratitude and touched by the depths of his love.

"Why don't we push the wedding up?" he said brightly. "Not the wedding per se, but why don't we just get the legal part done? Why wait for you to become my wife? Let's just go to the courthouse or county clerk or whatever. What do you think about that?"

What could she say to him after all of that but yes?

And now here she was, heading for the elevator in the building where she would become Stanley's wife.

But was she doing the right thing after all?

As the elevator ascended, Stanley grabbed her hand, his face full of love and contentment.

She smiled back at him.

I'm doing the right thing. I'm doing the right thing...

***

Everyone's eyes went to Brandon immediately, but Erica didn't notice he had everyone's attention until later.

When Brandon suddenly materialized in the room, he was all she could see—his familiar frame catching her attention easily.

Then, when his eyes found hers, they were all she could focus on.

She was released from their captivity only when the blue-tipped orbs turned from her to settle on someone else.

"I'm sorry, Stanley," he said, looking truly apologetic. "But I can't let this happen."

Brandon now had all the clerks' attention too, but no one seemed to mind the interruption in the processing.

By now, everyone had probably sensed an impending drama, and no one wanted to miss it. For some people, moments like these were what they lived for.

"Brandon!" Erica said, nervously. "How did you find me?"

Why was that question the first thing out of her mouth?

She hoped he didn't mention how easy she had made it for him, blabbing to his twin about the details.

"You know I have the resources to do so anytime I want," he said with a deliberate look. "And it looks like I caught you right in time. Erica, I love you. Far beyond how I loved you before. I don't just love you as the best friend who has always been there for me, I love you as a woman I want to always be there for me, every day, at my side for the rest of my life. And I want to be there for you the same way. Erica, I want you to be my leading lady. I love the woman you've grown into—that awkward, shy, sweet girl turned into a beautiful, confident woman. Still sweet, still looking at me like that—the way you are now. You can't deny it, Erica, and I know the issue isn't whether or not there's love here between us; we definitely have that in common—love for each other. I don't doubt you love Stanley, but that love is no match for ours. Don't deny me the chance to show you how much I've grown since you last saw me years ago, and how much more capable I am of loving you the way you need to be."

"But you said yourself that, sometimes, love isn't enough. Why should I care in your case, but not Stanley's?"

"Because there's one major difference between me and Stanley when it comes to this. I'm sure he loves you too, and I'm not here to try to figure out or compare who loves you more—perhaps we both need you equally—but the difference is, I know I make you feel alive. There's no lukewarm love here—we burn for each other."

He took a few steps toward them, and Stanley stood up, the action distracting her long enough to regain her composure from Brandon's sudden nearness.

Stanley looked from her to Brandon, and then back again.

"Erica," he finally said, turning fully toward her and offering her his hands. She took them and he searched her eyes.

Erica found herself unable to utter a single word. She

could only stare back at him while trying to ignore the burn of Brandon's blue gaze.

"Do you love him?" Stanley asked softly, his voice almost a whisper.

Erica considered lying then figured it was useless.

She nodded her head, closing her eyes briefly. Then she quickly said, "But I don't want to be with him. I want to be with you."

Stanley shook his head slowly, a sad smile forming on his face. "Like I said, I've had a lot more experience, and you can lie to yourself all you want, but I know this is a losing game. I was willing to try anyway; I fooled myself into thinking that if I could just convince you to physically stay away from him, you'd be mine again. But I see you were never really mine, were you? You always belonged to him."

He let out a breath. "I can't compete with that. I see the way you guys are looking at each other even now. Your story's long from over, and I was a fool to think you had closed a chapter when..." He stopped. "I will always love you, Erica, and as much as I want to selfishly keep you to myself, I know how unhappy it will make you, and that in the long run, it will work against me. I love you enough that I can't stand to be a part of your misery, and I know you'll be miserable if I insist you never see him again. I know you'll do it for me, but it would be for no one's good, and the only reason I'd ask it is because we all know what'll happen if you two come together in person; I'm powerless to stop it."

Stanley looked at Brandon. "Looks like I have to

adopt your philosophy for this one, Brandon, and go with the flow; no use fighting this current."

Stanley kissed her hands then dropped them, and then headed for the exit.

Watching his back, dejection all over him, Erica's heart tugged.

She knew she couldn't make it better, but she was moved anyway.

"Stanley, wait!" she said, about to go after him, but Brandon grabbed her arm, stopping her and effectively forcing her to look at him.

"You know he's right," he said. "There's no stopping this."

His gaze burned into hers.

Everything in her began to melt, and Stanley quickly became a distant memory. All she could see was Brandon, and, lost in the pool of his eyes, she could deny him nothing—definitely not the kiss he was about to plant on her as his lips came toward hers.

She was powerless against the way he made her heart slam her chest, the way he sent her body tingling, the way he sent her emotions haywire. All she wanted was his lips on hers, his arms around her, to feel pressed against him. She wanted his voice in her ear, whispering whatever. She longed to drown in those eyes trained on her.

He broke the kiss temporarily to say, "I love you," and she sure as hell couldn't resist saying, "I love you" back before their lips met again.

When they finally pulled away, they eventually remembered where they were when applause suddenly exploded all around them.

Erica felt like she had just given the best performance of her life, despite not a single part of what had transpired before being an act.

They both smiled at the grinning people in the room, including the faces lit up behind the glass.

When Erica looked back at Brandon, his gaze had become even more intense.

A thought crossed her mind, and she realized that Brandon had probably been thinking the same thing.

CHAPTER 12

ENDLESS SUMMER

"Okay, now that we've got our marriage license, how and when do we make it official?" Brandon asked eagerly.

"We can go downstairs and finish up there with a quick ceremony. That's what I...had planned originally. Or we could wait a few months and throw a real wedding and have everything made official then."

"I want to marry you now, Erica. Right now. I want to make you my wife and I don't want to wait another moment," he said, grabbing her hands. "I need your acceptance of me as the man who will take care of you and look after you for the rest of your life. I know our family's not here or anything, and you probably want your mom here, and I'd love to have Alec and Connor and my mom here, but we don't have to tell anyone just yet. We can just tell everyone we got engaged and then throw the big wedding later. What do you say?"

Erica smiled, her eyes wet. "You read my mind. Let's do it," she said. "But just so you know, we need a witness. I hired someone from the street to act as a witness earlier—guess we can still use him." She grinned.

Brandon considered his prospects. He couldn't think of anyone he trusted to have discretion plus get down there fast enough. He even considered calling Connor up for a moment, but Connor wasn't the greatest with secrets.

"Deal," he said. "Bring 'cousin Skeeter' or whoever the random is on down. Let's do this."

***

AFTER THEIR QUICKIE CEREMONY, they spent most of the rest of the day locking lips and at least part of the day at Brandon's place, reacquainting themselves with each other's bodies.

The first person Brandon called when they came up for air was Connor.

Brandon could barely contain his excitement and had to keep checking himself, reminding himself not to let the big news slip.

"Connor, it worked! I got her back—Erica and I are engaged now."

"Sweet!" Connor said. "I knew it would happen. I'm so glad for you, bro; I hope being with her is all you wanted and more. Can't wait to see her and say hi. She still has that frizzy-ass hair?"

Brandon laughed. "Her hair has multiple

personalities and I love each one. She's amazing, Connor. God, I hope you get to feel this way about someone someday."

"Okay, stop right there. Don't try to marry me off—I'm still far too young for that."

"Yeah, well I thought I was too. But if the one who does this to you crosses your path, don't let her go. Anyway, when the time comes, you'll see."

As soon as he hung up from Connor, Brandon glanced over at Erica and then called Alec when he saw her on her cell phone in her own world. He figured she was probably spreading the news of their 'engagement' herself, talking to her mom, first.

He focused on Alec once he heard his big brother's voice.

Alec congratulated him and then asked him about the date.

"We haven't decided yet. Hey, what do you think of a double wedding?"

Alec laughed. "I don't think Dahlia will go for it. Besides, I don't feel like sharing her that day anyway. And I want her to have her sparkling moment solo."

"So neither of you will go for it is what you're saying," Brandon said, smiling.

"I guess so. But I'd bet your girl doesn't want to share the big day either—just a hunch. Did you even run this by her?"

"No."

Alec laughed again. "You'll learn."

Brandon looked over at Erica again, who, at that

moment, had thrown her head back in laughter, and all he could do was stare at her beauty and wonder at his luck.

* * *

Erica looked amazingly right in his condo.

She didn't have a whole lot of stuff, so moving her in didn't even take a U-Haul since she basically only came with clothes, shoes, and books.

Stanley made himself scarce the day she came to clear out her stuff, and Brandon could tell she still felt bad for what she had done to him, but he knew with each passing moment that her sadness would shrink and be replaced by equal or double parts joy.

Now that she was here with him, married to him, and looking crazy sexy in one of his T-shirts, Brandon still couldn't believe his eyes and all that had transpired over the past several months.

He also looked forward to their upcoming movie nights—he had promised to watch a video of her first big play, and she had promised to sit through his rough-cut documentary.

They both eagerly looked forward to screening the movie they'd made a decade ago; Brandon had dug it up in one of his storage facilities.

"Erica Wilde," he said. "What do you think about a double wedding with Alec and his woman?"

She gave him a look that answered him clearly.

"Okay, how about we skip the whole thing? The most

important part is done, and you know what? I don't even care about making a big event of it—I already have everything I want."

She walked slowly over to him with a small smile, and then kissed him on the forehead.

"Yet another thing we don't have in common, it seems, because I care about a big event very much. Don't worry, I'll do the planning—you just show up in whatever I pick out for you. I'm having that wedding I imagined back when I was fourteen, Brandon Wilde."

He grinned at her. She could have whatever the hell she wanted.

Brandon watched her staring back at him, loving the way she seemed to get trapped by his gaze sometimes—like she couldn't take her eyes off of him even if someone pushed her.

"With whom did you imagine this wedding?" he said in faux-outrage.

Her smile widened and her cheeks flushed a bit. "Who do you think?"

Brandon felt a warm tingle pass through his body from the top of his head to the tip of his toes, despite already knowing the answer before asking the question.

"Anyway," Erica continued, "the first thing I want to sort out is where we'll have it."

Brandon thought about it for a second.

Then he said, "So I've got this gorgeous beach house in Hawaii..."

END

Check out Connor's story next! Excerpt coming up.

Visit Rose's author page at your favorite retailer for her full catalogue!

EXCERPT

CONNOR: THE WILDE BROTHERS

SYNOPSIS: Connor feels destined to live in the extreme, so he expects nothing more than drama when the latest annual game he plays with his brothers requires that he revisit part of his crazy past. He is compelled to face Gabriela Miller again—a girl whose heart he crushed in high school, and who would probably slap him silly if she ever saw him again. But Connor feels a pull to her he can't deny. Besides, what he did to her—that was so long ago; she couldn't possibly still be holding a grudge, right?

* * *

CHAPTER ONE - CONNOR

Gabriela.

The name followed Connor around, teasing him softly whenever loneliness threatened to overwhelm him.

It was a name he attempted to drown out quickly with a new, soft body.

Gabriela.

The name had first become a song in his head years ago, hitting him suddenly, but by then it was too late—Gabriela had been lost to him.

Gabriela.

It was difficult for Connor to pretend that he didn't secretly enjoy the idea of revisiting the past when Alec proposed this year's romantic challenge; he could barely restrain himself at the thought of having an excuse to revisit Gabriela, to get the chance to have those beautiful brown eyes of hers look at him in love and adoration instead of pain and hatred.

"Let's do it," Connor said eventually, after putting on a good show of distaste for the terms his brother had laid out. "The Hometown Hottie."

Let the conquering begin.

Connor had to resist the urge to rub his hands together.

"Here's the twist," Alec had said. "You have to wait two weeks before sleeping with her. And whoever gets her to say 'I love you' first and still stays with her at least three months after, wins the title to this beach house."

Challenge accepted—although getting Gabriela to say those words to him, considering their history, would make this challenge infinitely more difficult for him than his brothers.

Still, when Connor thought about contacting Gabriela, it wasn't the thought of Alec's beach house that danced in his mind as a delicious possibility of owning, as much as he loved it; it wasn't the beach house he desired most, he discovered to his surprise. He really wanted a second chance with Gabriela and looked forward to getting that chance.

How hard would it be, really? He was more than ten times the guy he was before—in more ways than one.

Besides, like he had told his brothers, "every woman desires to be a high-class prostitute—to sell herself to the highest bidder in exchange for a life of luxury; a life every woman is born or conditioned to think she deserves. A life we—the providers and protectors—owe her, the princess or queen she thinks she is."

This annual challenge of theirs was hardly ever a real challenge—not when it came to getting whatever type of girl they had decided on that year. It was always just a matter of which one of them would complete the task first.

* * *

Gabriela.

Connor remembered the first time he saw her. He had noticed the blond girl she was walking down the hallway with first but quickly dismissed that girl as a candidate for his plan. He needed to stay away from all blondes for a bit—all they did was make him think about his ex, Courtney, again, no matter how little they actually looked like her; in fact, the only person who really looked like her was her twin, but there were a few cute, blue-eyed blondes who looked close enough. Too dangerous. Slippery slope.

"Why don't you go for someone ethnic?" his friend, Tim had said jokingly when he pointed out a brunette that Connor still thought reminded him of Courtney. At least Tim hadn't started looking at him like he was crazy since nearly every girl he picked out for Connor got a shake of his head for the same reason. "Go ahead, I dare you. That should get you out of the zone. Man, you have the pick of the litter here. Show Court she didn't mean that much to you; show her you moved on. I know that's not true, but don't let her see you still moping like this."

"I'm not moping!"

"Dude, it's so obvious. She got you, man. Now, get her back. Grab another chick fast."

Connor considered the proposition.

If Tim had picked up on his broken spirit, surely others had, and he couldn't go down like that. Before Courtney, he and his brother practically ruled the school, and like Tim said, had their pick of the litter.

He only picked Courtney in the first place because she seemed the obvious choice—she and her sister were the female equivalents of him and his brother, and the sisters had guys aplenty panting after them. Since both sets of twins were at the top of their food chains, naturally, they should get together. Besides, he wanted the person he lost his virginity to be memorable.

Brandon had his doubts in the beginning.

"Maybe we should practice, first," Brandon said. "You know, before we..."

Connor thought about it. In theory, it was a better plan—take a couple of those girls looking at them with stars in their eyes for a ride and work on their lovemaking skills for when the time came with the twins. The only problem was that the other girls would no doubt share their experiences, and whether they liked it or not, Courtney and Tara might get word of it. Maybe sleeping with commoners before them would turn them off; maybe they'd turn their cute little noses up at having sloppy seconds.

Ultimately, Connor decided not to take the risk and figured maybe watching porn could help his moves.

Heck, maybe the twins were virgins too and wouldn't really know the difference. Even if they weren't, maybe they'd be understanding, and their relationships would last long enough that he'd get plenty of time to practice and get better.

Besides, what would his dad say?

Son, what the hell are you doing thinking about starting from the bottom when you could start from the top?

There was no question what he should do, so he decided to go for Courtney. What he didn't expect was to fall in love with her, and when she left him, he was crushed.

Now here he was, struggling to pick up the pieces again.

"It'll help you get over her," Tim insisted. "There's plenty of fish in the sea—you'll see she's not that special soon enough. Just keep trying girls out. Another one will bite you soon enough." He paused for a moment. "I was eavesdropping on my sister and a friend she had over. My sister also got her heart broken recently, and her friend told her, 'the best way to get over your old guy is to get under a new one.' Same concept here—fuck Courtney out of your system."

Connor surveyed the girls passing by.

They're all suckers, Connor thought as confidence tentatively made its way through him again. *They're all sitting ducks.*

Then he thought about his dad again.

Sorry, pap, but to get to the top, sometimes you have to start at the bottom. You know all about that.

Now to add to the challenge, Tim had him looking outside of his usual zone.

Someone ethnic? What the hell did that even mean? Although Connor's eyes always got caught on blondes first, as he quickly dismissed Gabriela's fair-headed friend, his eyes settled on Gabriela.

This must be what Tim meant.

He couldn't quite tell what she was—she was fair-skinned and had long, dark hair and dark eyes, but her features were definitely unique in a way that suggested 'other.' Was she Latina? Mixed white and Mexican perhaps? Either way, she was cute and he felt attracted enough to pick her as the first victim for his plan. Plus, she, too, looked at him with those goo-goo eyes.

Getting Gabriela to be with him was the easiest thing he had ever done; she seemed so grateful to be in second place.

Connor was aware that the school had been buzzing again about his recently single status, but he hadn't really noticed the hope in so many eyes until Tim pointed it out.

Now that he was with Gabriela, he saw a bunch of

longing and envious looks thrown in her direction, looks she seemed to revel in. And he still saw a few girls bold enough to look at him like Gabriela wasn't there next to him.

I've got something for you, they said with their eyes, and Connor didn't know what they wanted—if anything—beyond one night in his bed, but he wasn't about to jump ship just yet; Gabriela had endeared herself to him a bit, and eventually, he came to appreciate her as a friend. He would do the respectful thing and let her down gently at some point, and they would perhaps remain friends while he had his fill of the promises in all those other pairs of eyes.

But things went horribly wrong.

Still, it had been eight years since that terrible time—she had forgiven him by now, surely? If she was still available, she would take another chance on him, wouldn't she? The way she had looked at him back then before he crushed her, now that they were both older and more experienced—and his wallets and accounts fattened—she had to find him alluring and attractive again.

Gabriela.

The last time Connor had heard her single-word song, he dug up her contact information but resisted making contact; instead, he found another distraction, a new doll to play with. Later, he realized that the girl reminded him of Gabriela.

Connor dialed Gabriela up.

* * *

"Hey, Gabby," he began and then cleared his throat. His voice had come out sounding too soft for his liking. "It's Connor."

"Connor," she repeated flatly. Then after a moment she said, "How did you get this number?"

Connor grinned to himself. "I have my ways. What are you up to lately?" he said, trying to sound light and friendly—as if they had remained friends this whole time.

"None of your business and definitely nothing to do with you."

Her tone had taken a definite turn.

Connor found himself caught off guard by the sharp pain through his heart at her words—like a serrated knife jabbed in and then pulled out. He hadn't felt anything like that since Courtney.

He forced a chuckle. "Well, that was kind of redundant, don't you think?"

"Okay, let me spell it out for you, Connor: lose my number. Again. What I'm up to these days is no concern of yours and I'm not interested in spending another second on you."

Connor started to respond but realized that she had cut the connection.

Harsh, he thought, looking at his cell as if he should see her name instead of his home screen. *Unnecessarily so.* What bug was up her butt? The last conversation they'd had hadn't been so terse, so nastily short.

When was that last conversation of theirs, anyway? About four years ago or so, wasn't it? Back then, Gabriela had answered sounding confused, and when he heard her soft, gentle greeting, Connor felt a rush of joy—he hadn't seen or heard from her since she left their high school.

"Hey, Gabby—Connor here. How's it going?"

"Connor who? You mean Connor Wilde?"

"The one and only. Well, maybe not technically. Anyway, how have you been?"

She didn't answer right away, and for months he had wondered what she would have said had she not settled on, "Just great, Connor! Why the call? To what do I owe the honor?"

He had almost giggled at her unintentional rhyme. He realized it was from nervousness. He cleared his throat again, fighting off the almost-giddiness. "You ran across my mind is all. We used to be friends back in the day, right? Just wondered what you'd been up to. I know we all went our separate ways, but I haven't totally forgotten you. Just checking up on you."

"Gee, thanks. Look, I appreciate the call, Connor, and I'm doing just fine."

"So are you working on that nursing degree? I remember you talking about it. I hope it's all working out for you."

"No, I'm not, but other things have taken its place."

"But you were so passionate about it if I recall correctly."

"I was passionate about a lot of things, Connor. Look, I've got to go. But again, I appreciate the call. You take care." And then she was gone.

Now here they were, four years later, and she clearly didn't appreciate his latest call.

He hadn't even done anything to her since that last

time; they hadn't talked since no matter how many times his fingers itched to dial her.

What had changed? Why did it seem like she was mad at him all over again? Hadn't she forgiven him by the previous call years ago? Her anger couldn't have resurfaced, could it? They were all adults now! She couldn't possibly still be that mad at him for what happened in high school, for crying out loud. Lots of girls had looked at him the way she did—how could she blame him for wanting to taste the rainbow? So what if sleeping with her had been part of a dare? They were all exploring their sexuality then, and growing into a man for guys—well, it was just different. Girls just became women, but guys had to prove their manhood.

Why did she like him so much back then anyhow? Wasn't it for a reason equally as shallow as any guy's? She didn't know him well enough to care for him as much as she'd said she did. They were all shallow back then—they were kids, and as far as he was concerned, Gabby was just like all the others—infatuated easily by some silly surface thing.

But he eventually realized how little it actually took to fall in love with someone sometimes.

He sighed.

For now, he'd just have to find someone else for the stupid beach house challenge. Time was of the essence...

Grab the rest of Connor's story from your favorite retailer!

ABOUT THE AUTHOR

Rose Francis likes reading and writing psychological fiction, particularly stories addressing difficult topics.

She has been writing from a very early age and is thrilled to have a platform that allows her to bring her tales to the public!

Visit Rose's author page at your favorite retailer for her full catalogue.

Contact:
rose_francis@live.com
https://rosefrancis.poisonarrowpublishing.com

MAILING LIST

To keep up with Rose's new releases and giveaways, **sign up for her newsletter by scanning the code below**!

OTHER WORK

THE BILLIONAIRE'S ASSISTANT

Stressed Naomi is having one of those "Murphy's Law" kind of days—everything that can go wrong is going *horribly* wrong. Traumatized by events from the night before, she ends up distracted at work—to the point that it gets her fired. Her continued distraction leads to more catastrophe as she almost smashes into a stranger as she hurries away—or is it a blessing in disguise? Noticing her distress, the handsome, wealthy-looking stranger offers her an attractive solution to her immediate needs: work for him as his personal assistant—no catch. Ha! She doesn't believe him, but her desperation makes her accept, and it isn't long before she suspects he wants a whole lot more from her than getting his coffee! She is used to saving herself, but can she resist the hunk who saved her?

The Billionaire's Assistant is the first book in *The*

Billionaire's Proposition series. Each standalone tale highlights the love story of one of three billionaire cousins.

SERVING THE BILLIONAIRE

Curvy Cherise never expected the hot new guest in her restaurant to request her as his server. He had so many other options—thinner, prettier types more than eager to cater to *all* of his needs. But the sexy, mysterious man insists on having the bodacious beauty—in more ways than one! Suddenly, Cherise finds herself facing all sorts of indecent propositions. What the heck is the handsome stranger really up to?

This is the second book in *The Billionaire's Proposition.*

THE TYCOON'S RELUCTANT BRIDE

Lonely Megan finds her life even emptier when her best friend suddenly passes away. But she ends up winning a much-needed island getaway and gets seated next to a hunk who is convinced she's destined to be his wife! Can the wealthy stranger convince her they were made for each other?

This is the third and final installment in *The Billionaire's Proposition.* It is recommended to read this series in order.

OTHER WORK

THE BILLIONAIRE SCOOP

When Maribel moves to New York to pursue a journalism career, she thinks life can only get better, having grown up in the Deep South, battling racism. But job opportunities keep slipping through her fingers—until an unhappy billionaire spills his woes to her in a bar and she suddenly has the perfect scoop to launch her career! But can she betray the handsome man in his most vulnerable moment?

Jim Craig longs for normalcy. The son of a billionaire and forced into the family business, Jim is now facing one of his worst fears—an arranged marriage—and takes off before he can go through with it. He seeks refuge in a bar and runs into a beautiful woman who tempts him to take a load off and spill everything. Little does he know, the beautiful stranger is a reporter, and they both might get more than they bargained for once their secrets come to light!

The Billionaire Scoop is a standalone interracial romance on the sweet side. It is the first book in the *Secrets & Deception* series.

THE BILLIONAIRE DEAL

When Judy's longtime crush asks her for a huge favor—to help him get out of a P.R. nightmare by pretending to be his fiancée—she can barely contain her joy. She thinks she finally has a chance to get him to see her in a different light—as something more than his best friend's little sister—but it soon becomes apparent her playboy crush has no plans to settle down soon, and certainly not with someone like her. Once the storm blows over and they part ways, Judy tries to move on from the heartbreak, but Scott takes a sudden interest in her again. After being burned once, can she trust her old crush has finally seen what's been in front of him the whole time?

The Billionaire Deal is the second book in the *Secrets & Deception* series. It is recommended, though not required, to read *The Billionaire Scoop* before *The Billionaire Deal*. All three books in the series are standalone interracial love stories, but it is best to read the series in order to avoid spoilers.

SURPRISE BILLIONAIRE BOSS

Vivacious Annie is bored—especially since her childhood best friend left their home state to follow journalistic dreams in New York, leaving Annie feeling lonelier than ever. But an unusual shake-up at work clears an unexpected path for her as she takes a handsome stranger under her wing!

To appease his strict father and ensure his billion-dollar birthright, playboy Chase must go undercover at one of his dad's companies and toil alongside the workers. Working closely with the beautiful Annie sparks something in him, and he must find a way to woo her without exposing his true identity. But Annie is a tough nut to crack, and he'll have to dig deep to win her over! When an outside party threatens his progress on *all* fronts by exposing his secrets, will Chase figure out how to keep both Annie and his inheritance?

Surprise Billionaire Boss is the third book in the *Secrets & Deception* series. All three books are standalone interracial love stories, but it is best to read the series in order to avoid spoilers.

UNEXPECTED

In the last forty-eight hours, Julia Murphy lost her job, her boyfriend is nowhere to be found, and she just got word that she's pregnant. Unemployed and suddenly single while carrying a child is not the way Julia saw her life, but here she is. What to do now?

Billionaire businessman Beckham Stone hasn't seen or heard from his business partner, Niles Addison, in over a week. So imagine his surprise when Niles's most recent mistress shows up at his office one day, demanding to know his whereabouts!

As the two try to find Niles, they must deal with the growing attraction developing between them while almost everything else works to keep them apart. Will they find their way through the tangled mess?

Unexpected is a contemporary interracial pregnancy romance on the sweet side, and the first book under the *Taking Chances* series.

A CHRISTMAS MIRACLE

Brenda hasn't spoken to her half-sister, Rachel, since Rachel stole her boyfriend, and Brenda hasn't dated since. Now, Rachel and the man Brenda once thought she'd marry herself are expecting a child, and Rachel keeps inviting her over to have dinner with them. Brenda has already turned down their Thanksgiving invitation, but she doesn't want to spend Christmas alone, yet she's not sure she's gotten over her ex enough to face the two of them as a couple. But then she collides with Alex—a handsome stranger in a coffee shop—and everything changes. Alex could be the answer to Brenda's dilemma—or will he bring more holiday heartache?

A Christmas Miracle is the first book in the *Holiday Hunks* series—unrelated contemporary romances taking place around a holiday or special occasion.

A VALENTINE'S DAY SURPRISE

When Alicia's cousin asks her to fill in for her last minute on Valentine's Day for a babysitting job, she is shamefully available to sub in, so she agrees. What she doesn't expect, as she shows up at the client's door, is a handsome, sad-looking father, and a quiet, but endearing four-year-old. And she certainly doesn't expect wanting to see them again once the gig is done! Alicia puts the jarring night out of her mind as best as she can, but her services are unexpectedly called for once more, and she starts suspecting the client wants her for far more than watching his kid!

A Valentine's Day Surprise is the second book in the *Holiday Hunks* series.

OTHER WORK

A THANKSGIVING DILEMMA

For Karen Miller, housesitting for her sister turns into a whole lot more when she discovers a newborn baby on her doorstep one night! Her nosy but handsome next-door neighbor stops by to probe about recent neighborhood activity, and the two eventually realize the child was probably meant to be left at his place instead. Now that he's suddenly a father, Brian Langdon asks Karen for guidance, and the unlikely pair soon discovers more between them than the tie currently binding them. But will it be enough when a different sort of trouble shows up at their doorsteps?

A Thanksgiving Dilemma is the third book in the *Holiday Hunks* series.

A TANGLED WEB

Kimberly Jordan never meant to hurt anyone. But once a DNA test reveals her longtime boyfriend, Damien, is her half-brother, plus she finds out she's pregnant, she will go to any length to hide her horrible secret. Unfortunately for Kent Davenport, he's the perfect fall guy for her plan, having recently revealed his love for her. But unfortunately for Kimberly, dirty little secrets always come out.

A Tangled Web is the first book in the *Dangerous Secrets* series—a series of unrelated, new adult interracial love stories where one or more of the main characters has a secret so big, it threatens to derail—or even destroy—their most important relationships, their personal character, or their entire lives. The secrets are 'dirty.' Scandalous. Taboo. Secrets anyone would be wise to remain tightlipped on. But in these tales, one way or another, that horrible secret gets out. Let the fallout begin.

CHRYSALIS

Chrysalis explores love and forgiveness as the paths of four college students from different worlds—two wealthy, white brothers and a pair of middle-class, minority best friends—collide. It is the second book in the *Dangerous Secrets* series.

TRAPPED

A Zombie-type outbreak has left Serena locked up, alone, and about to die of starvation. Her husband took off to find food for them and never returned, but her husband's best friend, Steven, soon shows up to her rescue.

Steven has had a crush on Serena for a while, and at the price of losing his friend, he now has a chance to be with her. Will he take it? Or will they remain 'just friends?'

Trapped is the first story in the *Bite-Sized Romance* series—unrelated interracial love stories with a speculative aspect (sci-fi or paranormal).

OTHER WORK

LEAP OF FAITH

Lisa is making her way through college, hanging on to a relationship she no longer wants to be in for the sake of its familiarity. Daniel is a fellow student—a stranger, and nothing more than a blip on her radar until one day, an odd, sudden ability changes everything, making her consider leaving her possessive boyfriend for him.

A novelette, "Leap of Faith" is a light tale of budding romance with a dash of telepathy, and the second story under *Bite-Sized Romance*.

THE LIFEGUARD

Regina Hartley has had enough. The demands of life have taken a toll on her, and, no longer feeling equipped to endure the strain, she decides to end it all in watery surrender. But instead of drowning to death, she finds herself being revived on shore by a concerned, handsome stranger, and after saving her, the stranger refuses to leave her alone. She realizes she doesn't mind his attention so much, and she finds herself more interested in what else life has to offer overall. But after saving her spirit, will the handsome stranger eventually disappear?

"The Lifeguard" is a *clean* romance novelette, and the third speculative story under *Bite-Sized Romance*.

OTHER WORK

PLAYING WITH FIRE

Janet Cooper has a small problem: dumping her unfaithful fiancé has turned him into a stalker continually begging for her forgiveness. She soon realizes her troubles are just beginning, especially since her new coworker, Eric, is an irresistible hunk, and she has promised herself a three-month hiatus from sex since her breakup.

Eric Anderson has a small problem: he has been hired to infiltrate Cooper Investment Inc. via its heir apparent, Janet, but once he sets his eyes on the beauty, it's no longer just the business he wants to infiltrate.

As Janet's ex-fiancé gets more and more aggressive in his pursuit of her, she turns to Eric for strength and friendship, sending her ex into jealous rages, and her hormones into overdrive!

Playing with Fire is the first book in the *Sweet Redemption* series—contemporary workplace tales.

It is recommended, though not required, to read *Playing with Fire* before *In Hot Water* (book 2).

Made in the USA
Coppell, TX
31 May 2023